Big Thicket Ambush

Ki reacted with the swiftest move of which his sharply honed reflexes were capable. In a series of lightninglike moves he shoved Jessie away from him on one side, then circled in his steps to push Fletache away on the other. Then he dropped flat himself just as a gun roared and a streak of red muzzle-blast spurted from the darkness of the opening ahead.

Ki's dive ended in the fraction of a second before the whistling slug from the rifle passed close enough for him to feel the breath of air disturbed by its passage. As he hit the ground he was reaching into his vest pocket for a *shuriken* . . .

Also in the LONE STAR series from Jove

- LONGARM AND THE LONE STAR LEGEND
- LONGARM AND THE LONE STAR BOUNTY
- LONE STAR AND THE MESCALERO OUTLAWS
- LONE STAR AND THE AMARILLO RIFLES
- LONE STAR AND THE SCHOOL FOR OUTLAWS
- LONE STAR ON THE TREASURE RIVER
- LONE STAR AND THE MOON TRAIL FEUD
- LONE STAR AND THE GOLDEN MESA
- LONE STAR AND THE RIO GRANDE BANDITS
- LONE STAR AND THE BUFFALO HUNTERS
- LONE STAR AND THE BIGGEST GUN IN THE WEST
- LONE STAR AND THE APACHE WARRIOR
- LONE STAR AND THE GOLD MINE WAR
- LONE STAR AND THE CALIFORNIA OIL WAR
- LONE STAR AND THE ALASKAN GUNS
- LONE STAR AND THE WHITE RIVER CURSE
- LONE STAR AND THE TOMBSTONE GAMBLE
- LONE STAR AND THE TIMBERLAND TERROR
- LONE STAR IN THE CHEROKEE STRIP
- LONE STAR AND THE OREGON RAIL SABOTAGE
- LONE STAR AND THE MISSION WAR
- LONE STAR AND THE GUNPOWDER CURE
- LONE STAR AND THE LAND BARONS
- LONE STAR AND THE GULF PIRATES
- LONE STAR AND THE INDIAN REBELLION
- LONE STAR AND THE NEVADA MUSTANGS
- LONE STAR AND THE CON MAN'S RANSOM
- LONE STAR AND THE STAGECOACH WAR
- LONE STAR AND THE TWO GUN KID
- LONE STAR AND THE SIERRA SWINDLERS
- LONE STAR IN THE BIG HORN MOUNTAINS
- LONE STAR AND THE DEATH TRAIN
- LONE STAR AND THE RUSTLER'S AMBUSH
- LONE STAR AND THE TONG'S REVENGE
- LONE STAR AND THE OUTLAW POSSE
- LONE STAR AND THE SKY WARRIORS
- LONE STAR IN A RANGE WAR
- LONE STAR AND THE PHANTOM GUNMEN
- LONE STAR AND THE MONTANA LAND GRAB
- LONE STAR AND THE JAMES GANG'S LOOT
- LONE STAR AND THE MASTER OF DEATH
- LONE STAR AND THE CHEYENNE TRACKDOWN
- LONE STAR AND THE LOST GOLD MINE
- LONE STAR AND THE COMANCHEROS
- LONE STAR AND HICKOK'S GHOST
- LONE STAR AND THE DEADLY STRANGER
- LONE STAR AND THE SILVER BANDITS
- LONE STAR AND THE NEVADA BLOODBATH
- LONGARM AND THE LONE STAR FRAME

LONE STAR
IN THE BIG THICKET

WESLEY ELLIS

JOVE BOOKS, NEW YORK

LONE STAR IN THE BIG THICKET

A Jove Book/published by arrangement with
the author

PRINTING HISTORY
Jove edition/October 1988

All rights reserved.
Copyright © 1988 by Jove Publications, Inc.
This book may not be reproduced in whole or in part,
by mimeograph or any other means, without permission.
For information address: The Berkley Publishing Group,
200 Madison Avenue, New York, New York 10016.

ISBN: 0-515-09759-4

Jove Books are published by The Berkley Publishing Group,
200 Madison Avenue, New York, New York 10016.
The name "JOVE" and the "J" logo
are trademarks belonging to Jove Publications, Inc.

PRINTED IN THE UNITED STATES OF AMERICA

10 9 8 7 6 5 4 3 2 1

Chapter 1

"I don't know which part of the day I like best, Ki," Jessie Starbuck remarked. "I get the same good feeling heading for home at the end of a day that I do at sunrise, when I'm riding out to the range to begin work."

"Starting a full day's work and finishing it gives me about the same satisfaction," Ki agreed. "But whether the job I'm doing is hard or easy, I feel almost as good at noon, when half the day's work's done, and I know I can handle the rest of it."

Jessie and Ki were riding at a leisurely gait across the Circle Star's southeast range, not wanting to press their horses at the end of a long day spent covering the range. Sun, Jessie's big palomino stallion, was still fresh, but Ki's pickup mount was showing signs of tiring. Ahead of them the bronzing sun was hanging low in the Texas sky, and behind them the clear azure light of the heavens was beginning to shade to a darker hue with the approach of sunset.

"I liked what I saw today," Jessie went on. "It's been a good winter, plenty of rain. We should send a bigger herd than usual to market this year, Ki."

"Yes," he replied. "The bulk of the work's done now until it's time to make the gathers."

Jessie tilted her head to look up at the clean blue brilliance of the sky overhead. She went on, "I suppose we'd better move a little faster if we expect to get back to the main house before dark. I hate to push the horses after such a long day, though. Sun's all right, but your horse still seems to be winded. I think it needs to be walked a little longer."

"It's had enough rest to be able to move faster now," Ki told her. "It just hasn't been worked enough lately to keep it in shape."

"Just the same, we'll take it easy for a little way farther," Jessie went on. She lifted herself in her stirrups and looked ahead, where a row of bumps, the tops of fence posts, was now breaking the flat rim of the horizon. "The line fence isn't too far away now. Once we get to it—"

She broke off, frowning, as the silhouetted figure of a running man broke the level horizon line. Jessie knew the rule of thumb that applied to judging distances on the flat prairie: A rider on a horse could see the terrain for a bit more than seven miles, while the vision of anyone on foot was limited to not quite four miles. She glanced beyond the running man and saw, silhouetted against the bright sky, the bobbing crowned hat of a second man, following the runner on horseback.

"There's something happening up along the fence line ahead, Ki," she went on. "Somebody—I suppose one of our Circle Star hands—is chasing a man who's running toward us."

Ki stood up in his stirrups to bring his eyes level with Jessie's. For a moment he watched the dark moving blobs of the two figures that were now outlined against the sunset sky, then he settled back into his saddle.

"We'd better speed up," he said. "There isn't any way of knowing what's really happening until we get closer."

Without any further consultation both Jessie and Ki settled back into their saddles and toed their horses ahead. A short time earlier they'd been riding at a leisurely pace, letting their mounts set their own gait at the end of such a long day. Even Sun, Jessie's magnificent palomino stallion, had been moving at a sedate walk after the hours the horses had carried Jessie and Ki over the Circle Star's sprawled-out range.

"Whoever that running man is, he's certainly got long legs," Jessie said as they began closing the distance between themselves and the runner.

"And knows how to use them, too," Ki added. "He's moving fast enough to keep ahead of that hand who's chasing him. But the horse will make the difference before it's over."

Even as Ki spoke, he and Jessie saw the running man glance over his shoulder. Then their jaws dropped in amazement as without breaking stride the running man leaped into the air, jumping over the barbwire strands and landing on his feet on the opposite side.

When his feet hit the ground he staggered for a moment, but kept his balance. After a quick glance over his shoulder at the ranch hand pursuing him he began changing direction. Now he was heading away from the fence, leaving the Circle Star hand on the other side of it.

"I don't think he's noticed us yet," Jessie said. "He's been too interested in keeping his eyes on whoever that is trying to catch him."

"I think that's Bob Grady," Ki told her. "But at this distance and with the sun in my face, I can't be sure."

"Now that Grady's on the wrong side of the fence, we'll take over," Jessie said. "I want to find out who that man is and what he's doing on foot, out here on Circle Star range."

Ki turned his horse in unison with Jessie as she reined Sun around at an angle that would intercept the running man. The fleeing runner saw them then for the first time. He changed course once more, and began angling away from them, just as he'd angled away from the cowhand, who'd now reined in and was watching as Jessie and Ki took up the pursuit.

Almost two miles still separated Jessie and Ki from the fugitive as they settled down to a space-consuming gait that soon began closing the gap between them and the runner. The sun was dropping steadily, and though it no longer stabbed directly into their eyes, its glow spread along the horizon as it changed from yellow to crimson. Now the runner was visible only as a silhouette. They could see nothing but his body swaying while his legs churned like pistons as he fought the losing battle to hold on to his lead.

To Jessie and Ki it soon became obvious that the fleeing man was tiring rapidly. His long legs no longer moved with the vigor that he'd displayed while running along the fence and during the first minutes after he'd jumped it. Now and again he missed a step and staggered briefly, fighting to hold his balance and keep from falling.

"He's almost at the end of his rope!" Jessie called to Ki as their horses drew closer and closer to the man.

"Yes. We'll catch up with him in a few more minutes," Ki agreed. Like Jessie, he spoke without turning in his saddle.

Once the man's fatigue became so obvious that they could see it at a distance, the end of the chase came quickly. The runner began swaying, his feet tripping over themselves now and again, his body leaning far forward now as he flailed his arms trying to keep his balance. Suddenly he lurched ahead, seeming to dive into the grass-covered ground, and fell in a heap and lay motionless.

Although the fallen man gave no sign of moving and made no effort to get up, Jessie and Ki did not slow their horses. Now that their quarry was no longer moving, in a matter of moments they reached the spot where he lay, his arms outspread, his face pressed into the waving grass, totally motionless. Jessie and Ki reined in a few paces away from him and dismounted. They walked up to his outstretched form.

"Why, he's huge!" Jessie exclaimed. "And from the color of his skin, he's an Indian, but I've never seen an Indian that big in my life before!"

Ki had dropped to one knee beside the strange man's motionless form and was feeling at the base of his jaw for a pulse. He looked up at Jessie and said, "He's alive, but his pulse is awfully slow. Hand me a canteen, Jessie. I'll see if some cool water will bring him around."

Jessie's canteen hung from her saddle horn by its short supporting straps. She lifted it and handed it to Ki. He cupped his hand to pour water into it, then supported the unconscious man's head on his knee while he splashed a few drops of the water at a time on his face. Jessie stepped a half-pace back to get a good look at the stranger.

"Have you noticed that he's wearing moccasins and not boots, Ki?" she asked. "No wonder he could run the way he did!"

"Yes, I just noticed the moccasins myself," Ki answered. "He's an Indian, all right."

"I wonder where on earth he came from," she said, frowning. "There aren't any Indian reservations left in Texas. Could he have come from New Mexico, or from Indian territory?"

5

"I've been asking myself the same question, but I still haven't come up with an answer."

With the man's head propped on Ki's knee Jessie could get a good look at his face for the first time. She studied his swarthy brown skin and prominent hawk-nose, his heavy chin and the lumps of jaw muscle protruding below his ears. The bulges were as large as a baby's fist and emphasized his race, as did the coarse, black, shoulder-length hair held close to his temples by a headband.

What surprised and puzzled her was the stranger's size. He was larger than life in every detail. His shoulders were broad, his chest both long and deep. His waist veed below his rib cage to slender hips. His legs seemed unusually long and his feet huge as he lay sprawled on the range grass. The fingers of his hands were twice the size of those on any man Jessie had seen before. Lying as they did now, half opened on the grass beside him, they seemed as large around as her forearm.

While Jessie was examining the prone man, Ki continued to splash drops of water on his face. After a moment the stranger's eyelids fluttered and opened. He looked from Ki's hand to his face and blinked, then turned his head and saw Jessie.

"Starbuck?" he asked, his voice a low hoarse whisper.

"I'm Jessica Starbuck, yes." She nodded.

"Ai-ee! Then I have reached the place I started for," the man said. His voice was no louder than a sigh, but it conveyed his satisfaction. "You will not send me away?"

"I have an idea you've had a hard time getting here," Jessie replied. "Of course I won't send you away, not without hearing why you've come looking for me."

"Then I can rest now," the man breathed.

The stranger closed his eyes, and though Ki shook him gently, he did not open them again. Ki looked up at Jessie.

"I think he's made up his mind to sleep," Ki said. "I still can't guess which Indian tribe he belongs to, but I've got a feeling that once he's decided to sleep, it'd be pretty hard to rouse him."

"But what are we going to do with him?" Jessie asked. "We can't leave him lying here on the ground, Ki. It's getting dark fast, and he's so big that I'm not sure we could lift him onto one of the horses."

"We'll think of something," Ki replied. "If we can manage to lift him, we can make a sling out of our lassos and—"

He broke off as the thudding of hurrying hoofbeats broke the silence. He and Jessie both stood up to look along the fence line. Though the sun had set while they'd been pursuing the stranger, there was still enough skylight to allow them to see the form of a rider coming toward them. Jessie was the first to recognize him.

"It's Bob Grady," she said. "I'd almost forgotten that he was after this man when we first ran into him."

"Evening, Miss Jessie, Ki," Grady said as he came up. "I sure am glad you two was on the right side of the fence to take after this fellow when I couldn't catch up with him. I got here soon as I could; I had to backtrack to the gate after I seen you taking out after him."

"I don't suppose you know who he is?" Jessie asked. "Or what he's doing on Circle Star range?"

"No, ma'am, I sure don't, Miss Jessie."

"Why were you chasing him?" Ki asked.

"Well, I was on my way to the line shack over at the east end of the range here when I seen him," the cowhand said. "He was cutting across towards the line fence, and I knew he didn't have no business being out here on the prairie, him on foot like he was."

"Did you ask him what he was doing here?" Jessie broke in.

"No, ma'am, Miss Jessie. I didn't have a chance to. Soon as he seen me he started scooting off."

"And you started chasing him," Ki put in.

"I sure did, but danged if he didn't just about outrun me. He might just've made it, too, if you and Miss Jessie hadn't been on this side to head him off after he jumped the fence. I'd've had to do what I just done to get here, head for the closest gate and backtrack. I sorta figured I could help you run him down, but you done that without no help from me."

"We didn't really catch him, either," Jessie put in. "He almost outran us, too. We were just closing in on him when he collapsed."

"You figure to take him back to the main house?" Grady asked.

"We were just beginning to work out some way of carrying him when you got here," Jessie replied. "Now, it won't be as hard to handle him. Why, a man his size must weigh almost as much as a grizzly bear!"

"I think the best thing to do is put him on Bob's horse and let Bob ride my horse's rump," Ki suggested.

"Yes," Jessie agreed. "We'll lash Bob's saddle on Sun's rump, then we can just sling this fellow across the back of Bob's horse."

"Suits me," Grady said. "Except that old Perk's been out there for a week now all by hisself, nobody but his hoss to talk to. I was supposed to be there this evening so's he could leave in the morning to come back to the bunkhouse."

"We'll get Frank to send somebody else to relieve Perkins," Jessie promised. Then she went on, "Now, let's stop wasting time and get this man back to headquarters. For all we know, he might need more care than we realize. He certainly acted strange when Ki and I finally caught up with him."

With three of them working, getting the horses ready and loading the unconscious man on Grady's mount took very little time, even though darkness became full before they finished the job. Grady swung up to ride postillion behind Ki, and they started out toward the main house, the starshine on the barbwire fence that led to the Circle Star's headquarters furnishing a thin, bright thread to guide them through the night's gloom.

Even though Jessie and Ki had covered almost half the distance to the main house and the buildings when they encountered Grady chasing the stranger, the ride was a long one, for the southeast range bounded by the fence they followed was the area where the huge ranch's main work was done. The southeast range consisted of a vast unfenced expanse roughly twenty by thirty miles in size.

There were several smaller ranges in addition, although these would have been called pastures on a smaller spread. The other chief working areas were divided into the breeding range, the calving range, and the nursery range. There were, in addition, several cutting ranges where horses were pastured and trained.

As their names implied, each range had its own use and purpose. The cutting ranges held the cattle while they were being separated and shaped into breeding herds or market herds. Most of the animals going into the market herds were steers. A few cows were included in the market herds, usually those better fitted for beef than breeding. Jessie's standing order to the ranch hands was to choose only the best cows for the breeding herd; it was the one that would provide the steers on which the huge Circle Star's future prosperity depended.

Once the breeding season was passed, the heifers were cut from the mixed-sex herds and turned out onto the calving range, where later they would drop their young. When the calves were old enough to be separated from their mothers, they were put on the nursery range to mature. As soon as they became able to care for themselves the calves were herded onto the southeast range with the rest of the herd. They would stay with the herd until they reached maturity.

Year after year, as the calves matured the market herds were formed. This took place on the range across which Jessie and Ki were now riding. The expansive, well-grassed southeast range stretched over so much territory that a mounted man in its center could look in any direction he chose without being able to see any of its fenced perimeter. After the roundup was completed and the market cattle cut out for shipping to the stockyards, the big southeast range became home to the cattle that would form the bulk of the market herd the following year. Then the endless cycle of life on a working cattle ranch began again, with the hands once again dividing the cattle into breeding herds.

Jessie's father, Alex Starbuck, had created the Circle Star on the boundless prairies of southwest Texas. He'd bought a number of smaller ranches to form the vast spread as a refuge and haven from the hectic world of business and finance in which he spent so many of his days.

Alex Starbuck had been an unusual man whose career had taken him from a small shop dealing in secondhand merchandise to the status of a merchant and financial leader. Starting in the small shop located in the deteriorating area of San Francisco between Chinatown and the bayfront, Alex had begun to deal in oriental art objects as a sideline. The sideline had swiftly grown into a major business, and at an auction sale he'd bought an old windjammer to use in importing his wares from China and Japan.

Soon after this venture developed into a success, Alex had foreseen the switch from wooden ships and sails to iron-hulled vessels driven by steam instead of unpredictable winds. He'd moved before his peers in the business world could act, buying a run-down foundry on the waterfront to roll out steel for the hulls of America's fast-expanding merchant fleet, then improving the foundry and expanding it into a shipyard at the time when the demand for iron-hulled ships was reaching its peak.

With a solid base in the foundry and shipyard the expansion of his holdings had been meteoric. When the recurring financial panics of the 1840s and 1850s sent others running for shelter, Alex Starbuck had the courage and foresight to expand his holdings. By the time the Civil War ended, Alex had been one of the nation's richest men, with timberlands, mines, factories, banks, and brokerage offices dotted profusely around the nation.

His meteoric rise had drawn the attention of an unscrupulous group of European business giants trying to take over the rich industrial base of the United States. When Alex's life had been cut short by a hail of bullets from the guns of killers hired by his business enemies, Jessie—whose mother had died at her birth—inherited her father's vast holdings.

At that time the Circle Star had still been in its final formative stage. For a number of years Jessie, with the help of Ki, had devoted most of her time to wiping out the group of European financiers, for with Alex's death she had become their target. Victorious at last, her father's enemies vanquished, she'd then settled on the Circle Star. At last she had time—with the continuing help of Ki—to carry out her father's dream and bring work on the vast ranch to completion.

Jessie had inherited more than Alex's extensive business enterprises, however. From him, she'd drawn the feeling of compassion for the weak and helpless who were foundering in a world that they could not fight alone. Now, as she led the little procession along the fence line through the quiet night, her thoughts turned to the mysterious giant, still unconscious, who was dangling across the back of the horse behind her, and wondered again why he'd come looking for her.

Chapter 2

In the light of a lamp turned so low that it barely dispelled the darkness and gave the bedroom a twilight hue, Ki sat looking at the man sleeping on the bed. The stranger had not awakened even when he was being lifted off the rump of Grady's horse, nor had he opened his eyes while being carried upstairs and laid on the bed. Though the bed was a large one, the man was so tall that the cowhands carrying him had been forced to lay him on it diagonally. Even with his head at one corner the stranger's bulky, oversized feet stuck out beyond the edge of the mattress at the bottom of the bed.

Ki had volunteered to stand watch during the night after he'd noticed Jessie's drowsiness while they stood looking at their mysterious visitor after Bob Grady and three other cowhands had unloaded the sleeping stranger and carried him upstairs.

"You're as tired as I am, Ki!" Jessie had protested.

"Not quite. But I'll catch up on my sleep tomorrow. You certainly wouldn't want our unexpected guest to wake up alone. There's no way of telling what might happen if he came to and started rampaging through the house."

"Yes, you've got a point there," she'd agreed. "But call me when he does wake up. I'm very curious to know who he is and where he's from and why he's come here."

"So am I," Ki replied. "From the few words he said out on the prairie, he seems to know English pretty well. We shouldn't have any trouble getting his story out of him."

Though Ki had dozed fitfully a few times during the night, the stranger had barely stirred. Now and then the sleeping giant had involuntarily moved an arm or one of his long legs, and two or three times he'd muttered something in a broken half-whisper that Ki could not hear clearly. At no time during the night had he opened his eyes or showed any signs of waking.

While Ki had his full share of the oriental philosophy that called for an acceptance of life's buffets as they occurred, and for rising above them with quiet fortitude, there had been times during his long night of watching and listening when his mind had drifted back to the past. The son of a Japanese mother and an American naval officer, a close friend of Alex Starbuck on temporary station in Japan, Ki had been born after his parents' wedding had embittered and estranged his mother's family.

When his parents had died, Ki had become an outcast, an Oriental gypsy roaming the Far East looking for an anchor. During his wanderings he'd found temporary shelter on Okinawa in the *do* of one of the masters of the oriental martial arts, and early in life had become adept in the skills of empty-hand combat. Later, during his restless roaming he'd mastered the kindred skills of using the few weapons of the oppressed common people in their revolt against the nobility's tyranny: the *bo,* or singlestick and the star-pointed throwing-blades, *shuriken*.

Then Ki and Alex Starbuck had met by chance while Alex was touring the Far East, seeking merchandise to stock his early import store in San Francisco. On learning that he was the son of his dead friend, Alex had offered Ki a job in his store. The job had soon become much more; as Ki absorbed Alex's business philosophy, he'd come to be the older man's confidential assistant and companion, and after Alex's murder Ki had remained with Jessie, to serve her in the same capacity.

Dawn, creeping into the bedroom where Ki was watching the mysterious new arrival at the Circle Star, found Ki still awake and vigilant in spite of being very sleepy. He turned in his chair when the knob of the bedroom door clicked and Jessie slipped into the room.

"Is he awake yet?" she asked in a low voice, gesturing toward the stranger on the bed.

"No. He stirred a few times during the night, but so far he hasn't opened his eyes."

"Would you like for me to stay with him while you have some breakfast? I saw a light in the cookhouse kitchen as I was coming up the hall, so Gimpy must be out there now, fixing breakfast for the men."

"Aren't you hungry enough to go have breakfast, too?"

Jessie shook her head. "Not yet, but you must be. You've been up all night—or I suppose you have."

"I dozed a few times, but there wasn't any real need for me to do anything. Our strange guest must've been very tired; he hasn't stirred a muscle all night."

"Out there on the range yesterday evening he certainly went to sleep faster than anybody I've ever seen," Jessie said. "I'd like to know how long he's been traveling to get here."

"Many days," the man on the bed said.

Jessie and Ki turned to look at him. The giant stranger was sitting up, stretching.

"Where did you come from?" Jessie asked. "And why did you come here to the Circle Star? But the first thing I'd like to know is who you are."

"I will answer your questions gladly, Miss Starbuck," he replied. "My name is Fletache, and I am of the Tonkawa people. But to tell you more will take time, and when I heard you talk of breakfast, I—well, I am very hungry. I have spent much more time than I planned in getting here, but I did not have enough money to pay the railroad to take me all the way. I rode as far as I could, then began walking. I did not understand how far I would have to go, and I have had no food since the day before yesterday, when I ate the last of what I was carrying with me."

"We'd better get some breakfast for you, then," Jessie said. "As well as some for Ki and me."

"Suppose I go over to the cookhouse and bring back enough for all three of us?" Ki suggested. "If we eat here in the house the men won't be interrupted while they're eating and they won't be bunching up to listen to what Fletache tells us."

"A very good idea, Ki," Jessie agreed. "We'll have our breakfast in the dining room downstairs. I'm sure we'll be ready to eat by the time you get back with the food."

Although Ki had brought back what he was sure would be enough food to serve all three of them generously, including extra-large servings for Fletache, he found that he'd underestimated the quantity the oversized Indian could stow away. He had to make not one but two trips back to the cookhouse before their unanticipated guest declared himself satisfied. At last Fletache pushed away his empty plate and leaned back.

"Thank you, Miss Starbuck," he said. "I have not eaten so well or enjoyed such delicious cooking since I left my home."

Jessie nodded in recognition of the big Indian's words, then she said, "Perhaps you'd better start out by telling us where your home is. I've been getting more and more curious about the purpose of your visit, and I'm sure that Ki has, too."

"My story's not a simple one," the Indian told her. "And I've been wondering since I set out on my journey how you would receive me, and whether you would even listen to me."

"I always listen," Jessie assured him. "My father taught me that listening is the only way to learn."

"It's largely due to your father that I came to you," Fletache said. "Though I met him only once, I was of some help to him on that occasion, and he told me that if I ever needed his assistance, I should come to him."

"That sounds like Alex," Jessie said. "But even if you met him years ago, you should remember Ki, who always went with him on his trips."

"True," Ki put in. "When Alex traveled, I was with him almost constantly."

"But you were not with him when I met him," Fletache said. "And although he did not mention your name, I know now that he must have been referring to you when he told me that he very seldom traveled alone."

"Let me ask you one question," Ki said. "You understand that I'm not suggesting that you'd be untruthful, but I'm sure that both Jessie and I will feel better if we have no reason to doubt anything that you might tell us."

"Ask your question," the big Indian said.

"Where and when did you meet Alex Starbuck?" Ki asked.

"Many years ago, when I was much younger," Fletache began. "Alex Starbuck occupied a cabin on the river steamboat which I was traveling on as well, though I was only a deck passenger."

"Where was the boat going?" Ki asked.

"From Austin down the Colorado River to the Gulf of Mexico and then to Galveston," Fletache said promptly, "where Mr. Starbuck told me he would take passage on a coastal steamer to Panama. Then he planned to cross the isthmus and take another coastal steamboat to San Francisco."

"Of course." Ki nodded. "That was when it was a long and tiring trip from Texas to San Francisco because the railroads were still trying to build a southern line across the Rockies."

"After so many years, you still remember Mr. Starbuck's trip to Texas?" Fletache asked.

"I remember several of his trips during the years when he was still making his headquarters in San Francisco," Ki said. "That was when I'd first come to America, before the railroads had finished building their tracks across the country. At that time I traveled with Alex only occasionally. Later on, when I'd mastered English and learned how to help him with his business affairs, I went with him almost every trip he made."

Jessie broke into their conversation to say, "I think you've told us what I was curious about, Fletache. Please, go on with your story."

"Of course." He nodded. "As I was about to tell you, the boat Mr. Starbuck and I were on suffered an accident— a snag on the bottom of the Colorado River ripped out its bottom. When it began sinking, it tilted on one side, and people on the side that was rising from the water had much trouble because they could not open the doors of their cabins. The doors were then above their heads, you see. I was a deck passenger, and I helped the crew get out those who were trapped. Alex Starbuck was among the ones I helped."

"Yes, I remember Alex telling me about that," Ki broke in when Fletache paused for breath. "But there was always a lot of work waiting for him when he got back to San Francisco, and he didn't go into a great deal of detail about his trips."

"At least you've satisfied my curiosity about how you happened to meet Alex," Jessie said. "And knowing his ways, I'm sure he rewarded you for helping him."

"He offered me money, but I refused it," Fletache told her. "It was then Mr. Starbuck told me that I should feel free to call on him if he could ever return my favor."

"That sounds like Father, too," Jessie said. She paused for a moment, then went on thoughtfully. "And that's why you've come here? Didn't you know that Alex has been dead for several years?"

"I was very sorry to hear of his death, Miss Starbuck," Fletache replied quickly. "But news of the great world seldom reaches the isolated place where I now live. I was already on my journey here when I heard."

"Where is there a place today that's so isolated you don't get news of what's going on?" Jessie frowned.

"If you will forgive me for not replying at once, I will be grateful, Miss Starbuck," the Indian said. "But where I now live is part of what I have come here to tell you. Perhaps you will understand better if I start at the beginning, which is many years before I was born."

"I certainly wouldn't want to keep you from telling me why you're here in the way you think best," Jessie assured him. "Go ahead. I'm sure Ki's as interested in hearing it as I am."

"Before I start, there is one thing you must know," Fletache said. A thoughtful frown took shape on his usually immobile face as he spoke. "What I have to say may mean more to you if I tell you in the beginning that I am the last of the Tonkawas."

For a moment Jessie and Ki sat in silence, frowning. Then Jessie's face cleared and she said, "Of course! The Tonkawas are one of the oldest Texas Indian tribes."

"We were," Fletache replied. "Though our ancient enemies, the Karanakas, were almost of our size. Now there are no more Karanakas left alive, and I am the only man remaining of my own tribe."

"I suppose that has something to do with you coming here to find me?" Jessie asked.

Fletache nodded. "Something that is very important. But I must begin at the beginning if you are to understand why I started out to find your father. I asked many questions at the beginning of my journey, and at last learned about the Circle Star ranch. It was not until I was almost here that I was told Mr. Starbuck was no longer alive, but I also was told that you, Miss Starbuck, were here. I almost turned to go back to my lodge in despair, but there was a voice that spoke to me and kept me traveling to find you."

"Tell us your story, then," Jessie invited him. "Both Ki and I would like to hear it."

"At the time my story really begins, we Tonkawas were a large tribe," the Indian began. "A tribe of fighters. And I must confess something else, because you will certainly remember as I go on. My people ate human flesh."

"Cannibals?" Ki broke in, frowning.

Fletache nodded soberly. "Yes. When we began to do this was a very long time ago. The oldest men in our tribe remember that we did so, but even they do not know how it began to come about. We were still doing so when the first white men came to our hunting grounds. They were Spaniards from the north. We fought them, and because we were a strong and warlike people and the Spanish were few, we beat them and they went away and did not return until many years had passed."

"That must've been a very long time ago," Jessie said when Fletache paused.

"They came when my grandfather's grandfather was but a boy," the Tonkawa answered. "And when they came back he had grown to become a warrior, but this time the Spanish came from the south, across the river that they call the Rio Grande. By this time they had begun to call themselves Mexicans, after they had taken away from Spain the part of the land they lived in."

"Which they'd named Mexico, the Republic of Mexico," Ki broke in.

"Yes," Fletache agreed. "And they built towns on our lands, and we fought them, for we did not want invaders in the country that had been our hunting grounds for so many years. But they had guns, and we did not. Then when others of your race came from the east, what they had started to call the United States, they began fighting the Spanish, too. And because they were fighting our people's enemies, our chiefs went to their leaders and told them we would help them."

"And did you?" Jessie frowned. "I don't remember reading anything about the Tonkawas in the history of Texas that I was taught in school."

"Not many of the white men from the east looked on us as good people, Miss Starbuck. Not after they saw our fighters eating the flesh of the Spanish we had killed."

"Well, I can understand that," Jessie said. "I'll admit that I'm a little bit shocked and surprised myself."

"What I have told you is true," Fletache assured her. "I

was still a boy then, too young to fight with our warriors. But I am the son and the grandson of a chief. My father and grandfather were there, and they are the ones who told me of this."

"I'll have to admit that it's a fascinating story," Jessie said, shaking her head. "And I'm sure there's more to it."

Fletache nodded. "Yes, there is. The leader of your people was called General Houston. He forced his men to fight side by side with us, even though they did not like us."

"And Sam Houston and his men won the war," Jessie broke in. "But I have an idea that your people weren't any better liked by the Texans after the war ended than they were when you were fighting beside them."

"You have the gift of understanding, Miss Starbuck," the Tonkawa told her. "Just as General Houston did. Now I am nearly to the end of my story, if you will listen to me for a short while longer."

"Go ahead," Jessie urged the Tonkawa. "It's one of the most interesting stories I've ever heard."

"General Houston was a very wise man," Fletache continued. "He knew that we Tonkawas would never be liked or trusted by your people. He also knew of a place that lay along the Sabine River, far to the east in the Texas Republic. People called it the Big Thicket. Perhaps you have heard of it?"

"I remember having heard about it, or reading about it," Jessie said, frowning. "But I don't have any idea exactly where it is or what it might be like."

"I've heard of it," Ki volunteered. "And it seems to me that I ran across some mention of it when I was sorting Alex's papers after he died. But that's as far as my knowledge or my memory goes."

"That you know so little of the Thicket is something I can understand," Fletache said. "Few people except those who live close to it have ever been to it. General Houston knew of it, for he had visited it when he was a young man. He found then that no one lived in it, because it was covered with a tangle of big trees growing up from dense undergrowth. Horses cannot go through the Thicket; anyone entering must travel on foot, and they can move only very slowly. The general told our chiefs these things, and they agreed that very few people were likely to enter it. That is why he gave it to the Tonkawas for a home, in payment for the help my people had given his men in defeating the Mexicans."

"So that's why nobody has heard much about the Tonkawas?" Ki asked. "Your tribe's been living in the Big Thicket all these years since the war against Mexico?"

"Not living," the Indian replied, sadness in his voice. "Dying. The Thicket was not a good place to live in then, but it was the only choice our leaders had when General Houston gave it to them. He did not know, and our chiefs did not know either, that the Karanakas had found the Big Thicket and settled in it."

Jessie nodded. "Your old enemies."

"Yes," Fletache confirmed. "But we Tonkawas fought for what the general had given us, and though it took us a number of years we wiped out the Karanakas. I was growing to manhood then, and my grandfather insisted that my father must send me to your white people's schools to become educated. I did not want to go, of course. I am glad now that I did, for I learned much."

"And from what you've said, there are people trying now to take the Big Thicket away from you?" Ki asked.

"That is true. There are big trees there, fine trees with valuable wood from which furniture is made."

"But you must have some kind of documents that prove the Tonkawas' right to the land the Big Thicket's on." Jessie frowned. "Surely there are records in the Land Office in Austin that show the land belongs to the Tonkawas."

Fletache shook his head. "No, Miss Starbuck. I'm sure that General Houston made such records, and I have made a trip to Austin to inquire about them. But the Land Office has moved several times since General Houston made his gift to the Tonkawas, and if the records are still there they cannot be found now."

Ki broke in. "I've been remembering things since Fletache began telling us about his problems, Jessie. Once, a long time ago, when I was helping Alex put his records in order, I ran across something that mentioned the Big Thicket."

"It was my hope when I came here that Miss Starbuck might help me with my fight to keep the timber cutters from destroying our home," Fletache said. "Now for the first time I am beginning to take heart and see some hope that our homeland can be saved."

"Hold on to that hope, Fletache," Jessie told the last of the Tonkawas. "When my father died it became my responsibility to take over his affairs, and certainly what you once did to save his life is a matter that I can't take lightly. Ki and I will do whatever we can to help you save your tribal home, and we'll start working on it right away."

Chapter 3

"Yes, Miss Starbuck, we got the note you mentioned, the one the governor told you he was going to send," the clerk said in reply to Jessie's question.

"And I'm sure you searched through your files to find how the ownership of that area of land in East Texas is registered?" Jessie pressed.

"Of course." The man nodded. "We did just as the governor requested."

"I'm interested in hearing what you've found," Jessie told the clerk.

"I wish we'd found something definite to tell you about the Big Thicket land you've inquired about," the man replied. "But unfortunately, that isn't the case."

Jessie looked at the shelves that filled the big room. All of them were packed with ledgers and thick packets of documents bound up with strips of the red fabric tape that all government offices she'd ever seen seemed to favor. On the floor, there were boxes crammed full of similar packets.

"It seems to me that you have enough papers in here to

cover every inch of land in the entire state of Texas," she said.

"Oh, we're well supplied with documentation for almost all the state," the clerk assured her. "But you must understand that the Land Office has been moved several times while the legislature was finally deciding that Austin would be the state's permanent capital."

"And I can see that your files aren't exactly what I'd call in good order," Jessie said a bit tartly as she looked pointedly at the paper-crammed boxes.

"What's causing our problem now is that every time our files were moved it seems some of the older surveys and land plots and pages from the permanent ledgers got lost or were mislaid," the clerk told her. "But we'll find all of them, if we keep on looking long enough."

"So as far as your records go, the area in East Texas that people call the Big Thicket is still public land," Jessie went on. "And anybody can file a claim for it."

"Subject to the usual fees, and squatter's rights that may never have been recorded," the land clerk agreed.

"Suppose some conflicting claims turn up?" Jessie frowned. "What happens then?"

"Whatever the Land Commissioners decide. It's their job to make the final decision. They'll usually arrange for a public hearing where they listen to the claimants and inspect whatever written records there are to prove which of them filed on the land first. Then the commissioners meet and study whatever has been put on the record, and decide which claim is valid."

"How long does all this take?" Jessie asked.

"Oh, three or four years at the least. Maybe longer. It all depends on what the written evidence shows, and the kind of pleas that the contestants have made in the final hearing."

"And while someone's trying to establish ownership of a piece of land, suppose a land pirate appears and takes it away from them by force?"

"Miss Starbuck, there are laws against that happening, and we can call on the Rangers to enforce them," the clerk replied.

"I see." Jessie nodded. "And since there's obviously no way to speed things up, I'm going to do some thinking about the best way to handle our problem without having to depend on either the Land Office or the Texas Rangers."

Leaving the Land Office, Jessie walked slowly across the spacious grounds that surrounded the capitol, her mind busy with the problems that still stood in the way of giving Fletache the help she'd promised.

Nothing that the clerk had told her was really a surprise. She still remembered some of the occasions when Alex had been trying to get clear title to land he'd needed to buy for his widespread enterprises, and especially the problems that he'd run into with Texas land laws during the years he'd devoted to putting together the huge spread that was now the Circle Star.

Reaching the end of the capitol's wide surrounding grounds she turned up Eleventh Street to Brazos. Another few steps brought her to the Driskill Hotel, its cut-stone facade still showing the raw scars of its newness. She went into the tiled lobby and stopped at the registration desk.

"Although I haven't noticed one, I'm sure you must have a direct connection to the telegraph company's office," she said to the room clerk.

"Of course, Miss Starbuck. If you have your message ready, I'll be glad to give it to the operator to transmit."

"I don't have it written, but I'll take care of that very quickly," she told him.

On the sheet of paper the clerk put in front of her she

filled in the name and address of Gregory Hendricks, the young attorney with whom she'd become acquainted, and who she still visited occasionally in San Antonio. Then she wrote her message. Like most of her telegrams, it was brief and to the point: *Need you in Austin at once to handle case. Jessie.*

Handing the telegram to the clerk, Jessie went up to the four-room suite on the second floor that she'd engaged for their stay in Austin. Ki and Fletache were lounging in easy chairs in the sitting room, talking idly. They abandoned their conversation when Jessie came in, and as she turned away from the door both looked at her expectantly.

"It's going to take some time to get this all straightened out," she told them. "So far, all I've been able to find out is that the Land Office books don't have records of any claims whatever having been filed on a single piece of the land in the Big Thicket."

"But we Tonkawas were given the land by General Houston!" Fletache protested. "And we have lived on it since it became ours! What are we—"

"Fletache," Jessie interrupted, "those men who've been bothering you about land rights in the Thicket may be the worst kind of timber pirates, but they're not likely to start cutting your trees unless they have some kind of ruling from the Land Office that will give them an excuse."

"How can you be sure?" he asked. The worried frown on his face that had appeared while Jessie was explaining grew deeper and deeper as he spoke.

"I can't be, of course. But if they should turn out to be timber pirates, they'll find themselves in a great deal of trouble. The law won't let them take your land away."

"From what I have seen happen in my life, the law is on the side of your people, Jessie, not mine."

"It's not going to be that way this time, Fletache," Jessie replied confidently. "You'll have the law on your side."

"How can I be sure of that?" he asked.

"I'll be able to answer that better later on," she replied. "I've sent a telegram to a lawyer in San Antonio, asking him to come here at once."

"Greg Hendricks?" Ki broke in to ask. When Jessie nodded, he went on, "Of course. I'd forgotten that he's an expert on Texas land laws."

"What do you expect this lawyer to do?" the big Tonkawa asked.

From the tone of Fletache's voice, Jessie could see that he was badly in need of encouragement. "Greg's a very ingenious young man," she assured him. "He's also an expert on the Texas laws concerning land rights."

"Then you believe he can find a way to save our homes?"

"As sure as it's possible to be right now. I think that Greg can find a way to get rid of the timber pirates forever, and I'm sure that whatever way he comes up with will also include settling your claim to the land General Houston gave the Tonkawas in the Big Thicket."

"Even if I am the last of the tribe?"

"Yes, of course," Jessie said, nodding. "I've had to learn a little bit about land laws myself. The grant's valid until no survivors of the tribe it was given to remain alive."

"That is what I have also been told," Fletache said. "But I have found that your laws can be changed when somebody with enough power wants land that was given to Indians."

"Unfortunately, that's been true in the past," Jessie replied. "The problem is that time has brought changes to everything, including the laws."

"But the land does not change," the Tonkawa put in.

"We have been careful to keep it as it was when General Houston gave it to my people."

"All we can do right now is wait until Greg Hendricks gets here," Jessie went on. "Then we can follow his advice. I'm sure that Greg will know the best way to go about saving the Big Thicket for you."

Jessie was waiting at the Austin depot when Greg Hendricks stepped off the train from San Antonio that evening. They greeted one another as lovers who have long been apart—with a bit of hesitancy on both sides. Not until they got into the hackney cab which Jessie had waiting and Greg bent to kiss her and she returned his kiss with as much ardor as he displayed did the invisible veil between them dissolve.

"I hope we'll manage to have some time to ourselves while I'm here," the young attorney said as Jessie snuggled down into his arms while the hackney cab lurched over the bumpy brick street that led to the Driskill.

"As much as we can," Jessie promised. "But I'm trying to help a very worried Indian who came to the Circle Star a few days ago. He'd traveled on foot all the way from the Big Thicket in East Texas because years ago he did Alex a good turn and Alex told him to call on him if he ever needed help."

"Your telegram said it was a matter of land rights," Greg went on. "I suppose the Indians are being pushed off tribal lands they were promised would be theirs forever?"

Jessie nodded. "Something like that. But it's quite a bit more complicated. Fletache—that's the Indian's name—is waiting at the hotel with Ki. And I've reserved a room for you directly across the hall from my suite, so we'll have as much time to ourselves as we can manage."

"I'm afraid it won't be a great deal." Greg frowned. "I

could just get a two-day postponement from the judge on the case I'm handling now, so I'll only have this evening and part of tomorrow to work on yours."

"At least you can get a start. And we'll have tonight to ourselves," Jessie promised. "Then, on the way back to the Circle Star—"

Greg's lips closing over hers cut off Jessie's words, and they said nothing more until the hackney rolled to a stop at the hotel.

"There isn't much more that I can do right at this minute," Greg told Jessie and Ki and Fletache. "The Land Office people say that they're still going through their records, and that's going to take time."

"How much time?" Jessie asked.

"I'd be foolish even to guess how long they'll spend looking, Jessie," the attorney replied. "It could be just a few days, but it might also be several months."

"Judging by the heaps of papers that I saw yesterday when I was at the Land Office, it could also be several years."

Greg nodded. "Yes. I warned you that getting the Tonkawas' title cleared might be a long job."

"Is there something we can do to make it faster?" Fletache frowned. "Those loggers aren't gong to wait very long before they start cutting trees in the Thicket. They were just going back to where they finished their last job to get their tools when I left."

"Somewhere along the way we've got to prove that Sam Houston intended for the Tonkawas to have the Big Thicket as long as the tribe existed," Hendricks said thoughtfully after he'd listened to Fletache's story. "He must've made a written record of his gift."

The Tonkawa nodded. "Perhaps he did. But if there is a paper of any kind that says so, I know nothing of it."

"Then, we'll have to do some looking, and I'll have to study the law books to see what legal grounds I have for doing what I've planned," Hendricks went on. "But the first thing I'll do tomorrow is ask for a court order that will keep the timbermen from doing any cutting in the Big Thicket. I'm sure I can get a judge to issue one, but that's about as far as I can see ahead right now."

"All of us can use some rest, I'm sure," Jessie put in. "So why don't we call it a day?"

They broke up then, Jessie, Ki, and Fletache going to their bedrooms, and Greg Hendricks crossing the hall to his room. Jessie took her time undressing and bathing, then slipped into a thin, clinging silk negligee. She opened her door a fraction of an inch and stood listening, then opened it wider and peered into the sitting room. It was dark and silent.

Feeling her pocket to be sure she had the key to the hall door, she stepped across the wide hallway and without knocking tried the door of Greg Hendricks's room. As she'd expected, it was unlocked, and it opened to her touch. A lamp with its wick turned low filled the room with a soft golden glow, and she saw Hendricks sitting in an easy chair. He was wrapped in a bathrobe and his bare legs and feet stuck out in front of him.

"I didn't want to say anything in front of Ki and your Indian friend," he said, "and I wasn't even sure you'd pay me a visit, but I waited in case you did."

"We haven't had time for a private word since you got off the train," Jessie replied. "But I was surer than you were, Greg. I knew you'd be waiting, and I certainly didn't intend to disappoint you. We've seen each other all too seldom these past three or four years."

"Only twice since we met for the first time in San Antonio," he said, standing up and taking her in his arms. "And that's certainly not often enough for me."

Jessie was unable to answer, for Greg's lips had found hers as soon as he'd finished speaking. They pressed together in a long embrace, their lips glued, their tongues entwining and exploring. Though both Jessie and Greg were breathless when their lips finally drew apart, their caresses did not stop.

Greg had slipped his hands into the loose front of Jessie's negligee and was caressing the firm pink buds that tipped her generous breasts. For her part, Jessie had begun stroking her lover's sides, her palms traveling gently in a long caress along his ribs from his armpits to his hips.

As Jessie slipped her fingers along his rib cage, she felt the small raised weal left by a bullet. The long-healed scar brought back memories of her first meeting with Greg, and how he'd aided her without question in escaping from danger, and had gotten the bullet crease from a revolver slug intended for her.

"It doesn't hurt anymore now, does it?" she asked, her voice low and soft, her lips close to his ear.

"No. And when I got shot that time, I think I was more scared than hurt. I was new to Texas then, and when those men who were after you broke down the door of the room where we were trying to hide from them, all I could think of was the danger you were in."

"But you did what was needed," she said. "I'd have been in a very bad way if it hadn't been for you."

"I'd have been worse off later if you hadn't taken care of that bullet wound I got. Why, that was the first time I'd ever really been hurt, or even in any sort of danger."

"But you did what was needed."

"I suppose. And I'm sure you remember how bashful I was when you began taking care of that bullet crease."

"You'd gotten shot trying to save me. The least I could do was see that your wound got the proper attention."

"And if you hadn't attended to it, we'd never have become lovers, I'm sure. There are a lot of times now, Jessie, when I think about the way we were—well, thrown together is about the only way I can describe it. And every time I think about that night, I realize how much I miss you."

Jessie kissed Greg's lips softly. Her kiss was not an expression of passion, but of thanks for what he'd done before. His recollection of the way in which they'd been thrown together brought to her mind the occasion of how Greg had stood by her during that dangerous encounter. She bent her head to draw her lips softly along the old scar. The memory of the past combined with the remembered faint masculine aroma of her lover's body prompted her to carry the caress still further.

She trailed her lips and tongue in a slow and shallow warm, moist arc down Greg's side to his hips. When bending became clumsy she dropped to her knees. Greg's hands were still cupped around Jessie's torso. He was stroking the soft, smooth skin of her firm buttocks and her sides and back, but he released her as she sank to kneel in front of him.

Her lips still trailing across Greg's abdomen, Jessie moved her head slowly to one side, stopping only when she felt the warmth of his throbbing erection brush her cheek. Now her attention was focused completely on his fleshy shaft. For a few moments she grasped the rigid cylinder in her hand, cradling it gently. Then her lips closed on it. She clasped her hands on Greg's hips as she heard him sigh, and she felt a small tremor sweep his body as she engulfed him. For the next few minutes she was absorbed completely in her caresses.

Greg's trembling continued, and after a few moments of Jessie's soft attentions it grew in intensity. Absorbed in pleasing her lover, Jessie was surprised when she felt Greg's hands grasp her shoulders and move her gently away from him.

"I've always pleased you before," she said.

"And you do now, too, Jessie. But I'm not as bashful as I used to be, and I want to please you for a while."

"Then do," she invited him.

Greg slipped his hands down Jessie's smooth warm body and lifted her to the bed. She dropped onto it and lay quietly while he bent to kiss her lips, then trailed his own lips down to her budded breasts. The soft, warm rasping of his tongue on their pebbled tips drew small sighs of pleasure from Jessie's lips, and her sighs grew in intensity. Then they became anticipatory waves of feeling as he moved his attentions from her tautly pebbled tips to the smooth contours of her waist and beyond to the downy mound and the inner nest that was waiting for him in the vee of her thighs.

Jessie did not lie quiescent, but responded as she accepted his homage, until his gentle rasping attentions set her to quivering and then to shuddering gently. The shudders mounted in intensity and after a moment she gasped and said urgently, "Come into me now, Greg! I want to feel you inside me!"

Greg was quick to respond to her eager ardor. He rose above her and she spread her thighs to receive him. Jessie gasped as he plunged into her with a single urgent thrust, and she writhed as he penetrated and filled her.

They moved as one now, rocking together in mankind's ancient rhythm, until Jessie's small cries grew louder and her body writhed more urgently below the lusty thrusts of her lover. Greg was gasping now with each full urgent penetration, and Jessie sensed that they were reaching emotion's peak together.

She heard a sigh of termination growing in her lover's throat, and then her own body took over as she reached her peak and trembled with its ecstasy. Greg was quivering also. He moaned softly as he lurched forward. His muscles deserted him and he lay quietly except for an occasional declining shudder while Jessie's spastic quivers faded into small, almost inaudible sighs of fulfillment.

Then they parted and both of them lay sprawled side by side in motionless exhaustion as the stillness of the night took over the room. They had no need for words now. Both Jessie and Greg realized that the night now belonged to them, and that they had all the remaining hours of darkness to spend together.

Chapter 4

"I hate to shift the work *I* should be doing onto you and Ki," Greg Hendricks said. "But the judge who's trying the case I'm handling in San Antonio would only give me a two-day recess. He made it very clear that I must be there when court convenes tomorrow morning, so I've got to take the five o'clock IGN train back this evening. But I'll put in every minute here until train time working on your case, Fletache."

Greg, Jessie, Ki, and Fletache were sitting in the Driskill Hotel's spacious dining room at lunch the following day. Jessie was across the table from Greg, with Ki between them on one side and Fletache on the other.

Greg went on, "From my experience with the Land Office clerks this morning, they're not going to hurt themselves looking up the files that cover the Big Thicket, so it's going to be up to us to do our own looking. Meantime, I'll get my correspondent here to file an injunction staying the granting of the timber-cutting permit that outfit's asking for in the Big Thicket. That'll tie their hands for several months."

"Suppose the court doesn't give you the injunction?" Jessie asked.

"They will," Greg replied confidently. "If one court doesn't, another one will."

"We'll just have to wait, then?" Fletache asked.

"It's not a matter of not wanting to wait, Fletache," Greg answered. "We need time to see if we can dig up that grant Sam Houston promised your tribe."

"We haven't had much luck here," Ki observed.

"No, but we haven't really started," Greg said quickly. He went on, "If you've studied Texas history, you'll recall that when the Mexican War ended and Sam Houston was elected president of Texas, the capital was in Houston, because that's where Sam lived. By the time Texas became a state, Sam Houston was out of office and a very sick old man. That's when the capital was moved here to Austin, but a lot of the state offices stayed in Houston for a while."

"Including the Land Office?" Jessie asked.

"Yes. And for a while the Land Office was in San Antonio before it moved here to Austin. And those offices never have closed," the lawyer went on. "Technically, they're just branch offices, but a lot of the old records have never been moved."

"Then you think the records of the grant General Houston promised my people could be in one of the other offices?" Fletache asked hopefully.

Greg nodded. "There's a possibility. And we can't afford to overlook it."

"But surely the Land Office would have records of all the land grants here in the main office!" Jessie protested.

"It's supposed to, but that's a long way from having them," Greg said. "Actually, there's never been a time when lists of every land grant in the state were assembled in one place. That's one reason why the cattlemen still have range wars."

"Then you're going to be looking through the records in the office in San Antonio?" Jessie asked.

"Of course. I'll put one of my clerks on the job as soon as I get back. And you and Ki and Fletache can stop in Houston and go through the records there," Greg told her.

"That has been done," Fletache said. "Motaki, who was the chief of our people when we were still a tribe, had a lawyer in Houston look. He found nothing."

"It won't do any harm to look again, I suppose," Jessie said. "And if you have a lawyer in Houston who works with you, I'd rather he did the job. You know that cost isn't any problem, Greg. If those timbermen are as anxious as they seem to be to get their hands on the Big Thicket trees, Fletache's place is at home. Ki and I are going with him, of course."

"I'll arrange for my Houston correspondent to do the search there, then," Greg said. "And my correspondent here in Austin will have one of his clerks go through the main files in the office here."

"All this searching is going to take a lot of time, isn't it?" Jessie asked.

"Of course," the lawyer replied. "But before my train to San Antonio pulls out this evening, I'll file a restraining order here in the Austin District court that will stop the timber cutters from going to work in the Thicket."

"Isn't that going to a lot of trouble?" Ki frowned.

"Not at all," Greg replied. "We might have to look at the records in all three Land Office branches, though. There's a good possibility the order conveying the Big Thicket to the Tonkawas might have been filed in any of them."

"We certainly don't want to leave any loopholes those timber cutters can sneak through," Jessie put in.

"These restraining orders you're talking about," Fletache said, frowning, "will they keep the tree cutters out of the Thicket?"

"They won't go that far," Greg explained. "They can still make surveys and mark trees for cutting, but they can't cut down even one tree in the Big Thicket until the orders are lifted."

"Then you think we still have a chance?" the big Tonkawa asked.

"Of course you do," Greg assured him. "The law's perfectly clear. In fact, we have two ways to move to secure that Big Thicket land for you."

"Two ways?" Fletache smiled. "That's certainly better than none, and I was afraid we had no way at all to hold the land when I went looking for Jessie's help. I would like to know more, Greg. What are these two ways?"

"One is enforcing the pledge that General Houston made your people, that the Tonkawas would always have a tribal home in the Thicket. That's the strongest one; but we need some kind of evidence to prove that the promise was made and is still binding. The other way is to have you file a counterclaim as an individual against the timber cutters. You've certainly got squatter's rights, living in the Thicket all these years."

"Even if we cannot find the paper General Houston promised my grandfather?" Fletache asked.

Greg nodded. "Yes, even without that. But somewhere, either in the Land Office records or the papers that're left from the time when Sam Houston was the governor of Texas, there must be some kind of written record."

"Then it seems to me we're in pretty good shape, Greg," Jessie put in. "At least we can keep the trees in the

Thicket from being cut down while the timbermen are grinding through this web of law you're weaving around them."

"That's our objective," Greg said. "Time is what we're fighting for, time to find the strongest position we can use to keep the Big Thicket intact for Fletache and his tribe."

"And time is what we're trying to help you get, so Ki and I are going on to the Thicket with Fletache. I guess you might say that we're becoming unofficial Tonkawas until this situation is finally settled."

A high-pitched, protesting squeal of metal against metal and the thudding of couplings woke Jessie and Ki. Then the buckling of the railroad coach and the shriek of the locomotive's wheels sliding over the rails on locked brakes brought both of them erect in their seats. As the Louisiana & Missouri Line train trembled and slid to a protesting halt, both of them stood up. They were joined a moment later by Fletache, who'd been asleep in the seat behind theirs.

They were still standing, exchanging glances, when shouts reached their ears from outside the coach. Within a matter of moments the outside noises were drowned by the excited voices of the other passengers in the car. The chatter and shouts inside the still-quivering coach grew even louder, drowning out the confusion of voices that still were being raised outside.

"What do you think it is, Jessie?" Ki asked. "A wreck, or a holdup?"

"It could be either one," she replied. "Whichever it is, we'd better go find out."

"Then I will go also," Fletache told them.

They started down the coach aisle, pushing gently past the handful of passengers who were just beginning to stir about as they realized that something unusual must have occurred to cause the train to stop. Reaching the vestibule, Ki edged in front of Jessie.

"I don't see anybody outside this coach yet," Ki told her after he'd opened the door into the open vestibule between the car they were in and the one ahead. "But you'd better let me go down the steps first. I've got a *shuriken* ready in my hand, in case we run into trouble."

"We already know it's trouble," she said as she stepped aside to let Ki pass. "What matters is what kind of trouble."

While inertia or surprise or fear kept most of the passengers in their seats, several men were following Jessie and Ki and Fletache along the aisle to the door of the railroad coach. Ki swung to the ground first and flattened himself out *Ninja*-style as a shot rang out from the darkness that surrounded the train.

Jessie's experiences in the disparate roles of attacker, victim, and quarry during the years when she and Ki had been battling the cartel served her well now. She had stopped in the coach door while Ki made his exit, and she held her position there in spite of the calls and shouts and shoving from the passengers behind her. As soon as Ki was safely out of the car she risked stepping out into the vestibule to peer along the tracks.

A lantern was bobbing now along the side of the raised right-of-way, and she could see the man who carried it and a second man beside him. Both of them were running along beside the cars from the direction of the locomotive. Lights from the windows of the two passenger coaches on the mixed train shed a dim glow on the area adjoining the tracks, and in the half-light Jessie could make out the shadowy forms of other moving men.

Then a short *rat-rat* of gunfire sounded from the engine,

and one of the men approaching shouted loudly, "All right, boys! This rattler's not gonna go anyplace now! Get in them passenger cars back there and find the ones we're after!"

"We might be the ones those men are after, Fletache," Jessie said, keeping her voice low. "But if they are trying to find us, I'm not inclined to stay here and let them take us."

"What shall we do, then?" the Tonkawa asked. "I have very little skill at fighting."

"First let's get where they're not likely to look for us," she told him. Her voice was calm and even. It held no hint of the irritation she was feeling for having put her holstered Colt in the suitcase that now rested in the baggage coach, out of reach.

"All the holdup men seem to be on one side of the train," she went on. "So I suggest that if we can, we get out on the other side and climb up to the top of the car."

Fletache motioned for Jessie to lead the way. She wasted no time in clambering up the iron rungs of the ladder at the corner of the coach and gripping the grab-bar on its roof to pull herself on top. Fletache was right behind her. For a moment they kneeled side by side on the roof of the passenger coach, watching the men running along the side of the train. There were three of them, all wearing long coats and masked with bandanas. The leader stopped at the car ahead of the one where Jessie and Fletache were crouching and swung inside while the other two continued along the right-of-way.

"I'll take this car, Cotton," Jessie heard one of the pair below call to his companion. "You go on down to the next one. If the Starbuck dame ain't in this car or the one back there where Biggar stopped, she's bound to be in the one you'll be heading for, so look sharp."

"Don't worry about me not looking, Tanner," the man addressed as Cotton replied. "But what if she ain't on the damn train at all?"

"Then we wait for the next train and search it. And we'll be paid for both jobs," Tanner answered. "Now git! We ain't got no time to lollygag!"

Without waiting for Cotton to move on, Tanner swung up the steps into the passenger coach. Jessie and Fletache heard a jumble of voices coming from the car, but could not make out any words. The sounds lasted only a few minutes before dying away. Except for the faint shouts that had started in the car behind them, and an occasional voice from the car ahead, Jessie and Fletache heard nothing more.

Then the rasp of of booted feet scraping on the iron rungs of the ladder at the end of the coach reached their ears, and without looking over her shoulder at the Tonkawa, Jessie said in a low voice, "He's finally thought about looking up here! Get ready!"

Fletache made no reply. Tanner's hat was visible now, rising above the car's roofline, silhouetted against the faint light cast by the locomotive's big headlamp far up the tracks.

Suddenly Jessie felt the Tonkawa's hands on her shoulders. He turned, whirling her around, putting himself between her and the outlaw. Jessie tried to break free, but Fletache pushed her down on the cartop.

While she struggled to get back on her feet, Fletache turned and took a step toward the outlaw. A flash of muzzle blast and the report of Tanner's revolver broke the night's darkness and silence. Fletache grunted and whirled halfway around as Tanner's bullet hit him. Then he shook his mighty frame as though to get rid of some minor annoying insect and continued to advance on the outlaw.

Then, beyond the moving Tonkawa, Jessie saw a flashing arc of silvery metal cutting through the darkness. It was Ki's *shuriken*, and the razor-edged throwing blade took Tanner in the throat. Tanner's gun barked and red muzzle-blast spurted through the night, but by the time the outlaw triggered his revolver its muzzle was pointing upward toward the night-dark sky.

Letting his weapon fall, Tanner closed his hands on his throat, but that was his dying gesture. He swayed for a few moments, still balanced precariously on his high perch, as the blood from his severed jugular vein gushed through his fingers. Then he toppled and plunged off the ladder.

"Are you and Fletache all right, Jessie?" Ki called from below.

"Yes. Fletache was hit, but it doesn't seem to've hurt him much!" Jessie replied.

"I'll be busy down here for a few minutes more," Ki said. "But I'll be back to help you as soon as I can."

Jessie turned her attention to Fletache. The big Tonkawa was holding his massive right hand clamped over his left forearm. He said, "I'm all right, Jessie. The bullet just grazed my arm. Let's go and help Ki."

"Ki doesn't need our help," Jessie replied. "We'd only be in his way, you hurt and me without a gun. Besides, there are only three of those outlaws left down there now, two if you take away the one up at the engine."

A shot sounded from the roadbed below. Jessie edged to the side of the coach's roof and looked down. Her eyes had adjusted to the darkness now, and the locomotive's headlight still glared at the head of the train, making visible the narrow strip of chalk-stone ballast. She could see the sprawled form of the outlaw named Tanner, and toward the engine there was another dead bandit lying draped over the steps leading to the coach ahead.

Ki was nowhere in sight, but as Jessie scanned the dark area beyond the chalk-stone roadbed she was sure that she saw one of the shadows moving in the gloom that hid the strip of land beside the rails. Then a light thud drew her eyes to the train's last coach, and she turned to see a man standing beside the back steps of the last car. He carried a lantern in one hand, his revolver in the other, and Jessie recognized him as the bandit that his companion had called Cotton.

As she watched, he raised his lantern and for the first time saw the dark blotches that were the bodies of his dead companions. He'd started running toward them when in the corner of her eye Jessie sighted a glint of metal. She turned her head to see Ki's *shuriken* arching through the night.

Cotton belatedly noticed the whirling razor-sharp blade, but did not have time to dodge. It sliced into the thin, fragile bones of his temple, and one of the needle-sharp points thrust into his brain. He let the lantern and his gun fall at the same time, but by the time his hands reached Ki's blade its edge had done its lethal work. His hands still clasping his head, Cotton crumpled to the roadbed.

"Are you and Fletache all right, Jessie?" Ki called.

"We're fine," Jessie replied.

"There's one more of these outlaws up at the engine," Ki went on. "If we could take him alive we might get some useful information from him."

"It's worth a try," Jessie agreed.

She started toward the ladder leading down to the coach vestibule, Fletache following her. Ki was waiting as they reached the narrow platform between the two railroad cars. He handed her a revolver.

"Here," he said. "The man who was after you and Fletache won't be needing this anymore, and it's still got two unfired cartridges in the cylinder. The outlaw who's up at the engine will understand a gun better than he would my *shuriken*, and we want him alive and talking."

Jessie took the revolver, and the trio started walking toward the front of the train. They concentrated their attention on the locomotive, ignoring the excited calls of the few passengers who were beginning to stick their heads out of the coach windows now that the shooting had stopped. As they reached the tender, Ki held out his arms and Jessie and Fletache stopped.

"Let me get on the other side," Ki said, his voice a shade above a whisper. "If we can take that other outlaw alive, we might get some useful information out of him."

Jessie nodded, and she and Fletache watched as Ki made a light leap that took him to the coupling between the tender and the baggage car, then dropped to the roadbed on the opposite side of the train. He signaled to Jessie with a brief wave of one hand and started forward, picking his way over the graveled ballast toward the engine as she and Fletache also began to advance.

Moving silently over the graveled roadbed proved to be impossible, even for the light-footed Tonkawa. In spite of their care and their efforts to tread lightly, the loose gravel grated underfoot as Jessie and Fletache edged forward past the tender.

They had gotten almost to the point where they could see into the engine cab when they encountered an especially loose stretch of gravel. Small chunks of it rolled under their feet and clinked against the rails. The light that had been spreading from the locomotive's firebox was suddenly blotted out as the remaining bandit moved to the side of the cab and thrust out his head and shoulders.

"Damned if you didn't take long enough, Tanner. Did you—" he began, then broke off and brought up the revolver that was dangling from one hand.

Jessie's shot rang out before the outlaw could trigger his revolver. She shot from the hip, but her lead went as true as though she'd taken careful aim. The impact of Jessie's bullet knocked him back against the side of the tender and his own lead thunked into the earth beside the roadbed. Then he pitched forward and landed facedown on the graveled roadbed.

Chapter 5

"I got to give you credit for being a right good shot, young lady," a man's voice said as Jessie and Fletache stood gazing at the sprawled body of the outlaw.

Jessie looked up. The man who'd spoken stood in the opening that led into the cab. He was leaning forward, holding the grab-bar that protruded beside the opening. He wore the striped denim cap and overalls favored by railroad engineers.

"You sure did do me and my fireman a favor by shooting that son—" He caught himself in time, then went on, "that train robber. I've been held up by his kind before, and I still got the scar on my arm here where the last one put a bullet into me, just out of pure meanness."

"You don't happen to recognize him, do you?" Jessie asked.

"Nope. First time I ever laid eyes on him."

"Did you ever see any of the men who were with him before today?" Ki asked as he swung into the locomotive cab from the opposite side.

"I never did get a real good look at the ones who were

with him," the trainman replied. "The one this lady shot stood with his back halfway towards me and the fireman. That didn't stop him from keeping his gun on us, though."

"Where is your fireman now?" Jessie asked, looking around the cab.

"Why, that outlaw fellow made him crawl back in the tender and lay down," the engineer said. He frowned and went on, "You're sure asking a lot of questions, lady. You know anything about these fellows that tried to rob my train?"

"No, but I intend to find out all I can," Jessie replied. "I suppose there'll be a sheriff in the next town who'll look into this robbery?"

"Oh, sure. Our railroad dicks will take charge of things when we get to Beaumont."

Fletache put in, "We get off at Beaumont, Jessie. The rest of the way, we'll go by boat."

"I'll wait and talk to your railroad police, then," Jessie told the trainman. "Now, Ki and Fletache and I will get out of your way while you get the train started again."

"Sure," he replied. Raising his voice, he called, "Frank! You can come back to the cab now! Looks like the shooting's all over!"

Scrabbling noises sounded from the tender, and after a moment the fireman crawled out and came up to join the group.

"I suppose this is the first time you've ever seen the man who held you up?" Jessie asked him.

"That's right, lady. But I don't guess I'll forget him for a while. He was a real mean one." Taking off his cap, the fireman traced his forefinger along an elongated red weal on his balding head. "He sure landed me one with his gun barrel when I passed by him."

"Did either of you recognize any of those outlaws?" Jessie pressed.

Both of the trainmen shook their heads, and the engineer said, "Outlaws come cheap here, lady. We're too close to the Big Thicket for comfort. That's where most of 'em run to hole up when the law's after 'em."

"You don't go through the Thicket, though?" she asked.

"No, ma'am," the fireman answered. "The line curves north a little ways after we get past Beaumont and goes north a spell, then cuts across on up into Louisiana and Missouri."

"And we've still got a ways to go to get to Beaumont," the engineer broke in. He turned to the fireman and went on, "Better go see if you can find out where the conductor's hiding. Soon as we pick up those dead outlaws and stow 'em in the baggage car, we'll highball."

"How far are we from the Thicket now, Fletache?" Jessie asked as the big Tonkawa shipped the oar he'd been using to propel the dugout since they'd left Beaumont. He laid the oar along the thick sidewall of the long, narrow craft as he replied to Jessie's question.

"Very close," he said. "This creek branches into a smaller one just a short way upstream, and we will follow it for only a few miles before we are in the heart of the Thicket."

As he spoke, Fletache was untying the rawhide thongs that held the dugout's push-pole. The pole was larger in diameter than a man's wrist, and longer than the dugout.

Formed with axes and hollowed with fire, the primitive canoe easily accommodated the three of them and their luggage. The pole which Fletache was freeing from its rawhide lashing was both heavy and unwieldy. The big Tonkawa was swaying and shifting in the narrow craft, which rocked and tilted from side to side as he lifted the heavy pole.

"Do you need some help?" Ki asked. "Your arm must be sore from that bullet crease."

Fletache shook his head. "I thank you, Ki, but my arm does not bother me. The bullet made only a scratch. And you have never poled a canoe, have you?" When Ki shook his head, the big Tonkawa went on, "I thought not. It is a skill you must learn, just as you must learn to ride a horse. Besides, it is not far to where we are going."

Their stay in Beaumont had been very short. The railroad police had been polite but firm in making it clear that they did not appreciate outsiders interfering in their business, and that they wanted no help from the trio. It was a repetition of the rebuff they'd received when they visited the Land Office in Houston.

At that time, Jessie had remarked, "You'd think they had something to hide, that our purpose here was to make trouble for them."

"Which it is in a way, I suppose," Ki had said. "From the looks of that office, the people in charge of it do nothing at all except draw their pay from the state."

"All I can see to do is to hire a lawyer here," Jessie had remarked thoughtfully. "A local man, somebody they might trust. I'll do that, and have him get his instructions from Greg. And perhaps it's the best thing to do, Ki. I know Fletache's anxious to get home to the Big Thicket. That's where we ought to concentrate our efforts."

Now Jessie and Ki settled down, Ki in the prow and Jessie in the center, as Fletache began poling the dugout up the broad, shallow creek. On both sides of them the land was flat. It showed the same featureless character that had prevailed since they had left Houston, the shortgrassed flatness of any area which for centuries had been sea bottom, brought to the surface by some great upheaval in the distant past.

As Fletache poled the dugout further up the stream against its sluggish current and into a smaller creek, the land grew greener, the grasses taller, and a few trees appeared. Then, as the creek made a sharp curve and they rounded it and looked ahead, they saw what seemed to be an impenetrable wall of green. Both Jessie and Ki stared in amazement. Their astonishment increased as the dugout drew steadily closer to the green barrier that rose so abruptly from the shortgrass plain.

When they were facing it even closer, the edge of the Big Thicket still amazed them, though now they could distinguish the characteristics of the individual features which formed it. Beyond an initial margin of waist-high green grasses there was a line of shrubs that grew head-high to a tall man, and behind the shrubs bushes grew twice as high before their identity was lost in the trees, which stood so close together that their branches intertwined.

Even the air in the Thicket seemed different as they entered the brush which formed its boundary. Unlike the clear air of the open prairie, that in the Thicket was moistly warm and lung-clogging. Then, as Fletache poled the dugout through the small gap made by the creek, the sun was blotted out and they were traveling in a continual twilight.

"I can certainly see now why they call this a thicket," Ki remarked as he gazed at the wall of dense, tangled, head-high brush that they faced on both banks of the creek. Above the seemingly solid green barrier the tops of great trees towered, swaying gently back and forth in a breeze that could not be felt by the three in the long, heavily loaded dugout. Turning to Fletache, Ki went on, "How big is the thicket, anyhow?"

"Very big indeed," the Indian answered as he continued

to propel the craft toward the mass of green vegetation with skillful strokes of the long-shafted paddle he was plying. He went on, "By the ways you use to measure the land, the Big Thicket lasts beyond this bayou for more than twenty miles westward, and it is more than that to where it ends in the north."

They'd grown used to the splashing of the broad paddle with which Fletache had propelled the dugout, but the pole he was now using never came completely from the water, and the silence that surrounded them was almost total except for the low, almost inaudible ripple of the water's smooth surface against the dugout's prow, and the muted humming of wind above the treetops.

A wide stretch of mucky, wet earth broken by the rippling water of a muddy little creek still lay between the clumsy craft and the beginning of the undergrowth. Jessie and Ki sat staring at the ragged line of small, scraggly bushes and thin, swaying reeds that stretched along the creek's banks, a tangle of brush and weeds that became taller and more dense before giving way to the untamed tangle of brush from which the thick-trunked trees rose, their branches intertwined above them to shut out any sight of the sky.

"Surely there are trails through all that brush." Jessie frowned as she studied the wall of living growth.

"There are deer runs and bear trails, if you can follow them," Fletache replied. "And there are also paths beaten by the Attacapas and Rasainais before their tribes died away. To find any trails in the Thicket you must look with the eyes of my people, and I do not think that will be easy for you and Ki."

"Aren't there other creeks like this one that we could go up with the boat?" Jessie asked. "It certainly looks wet enough."

"There are creeks, yes," Fletache replied. "And springs, too. But many of the creeks are little more than threads, too narrow and too shallow for even the smallest boat. And around almost all the places where springs rise and creeks run there is much deep mud into which you can sink."

"Then you're saying that a boat can't get very far up whatever creeks there are," Ki put in.

"That is right, Ki," the Tonkawa agreed. "But it is not as bad as it looks. Over most of the Big Thicket the earth is dry and solid underfoot. Only where the creeks run and the springs rise from the earth is the ground muddy and soft."

"How've your people managed to get along in a place like this, Fletache?" Jessie asked.

"It has not been easy, but it was a safe place for our tribe to live. New settlers coming from the east did not want to build cabins in such a wild place as this."

"So they passed it up and went on, I suppose." Jessie nodded. "Looking for land that would be easier to farm."

"Most of them did," the Tonkawa answered. "After they had gone into the Thicket only a short distance and found what it is like. So our tribe was left in peace. And the hunting was good, better than it is now, and we were sure the land was to be ours forever, so we stayed."

"Even with all the game to eat, it must have been hard for them to get along," Jessie observed.

Fletache nodded soberly. "From the stories that the oldest of the Tonkawas told before they died, it was very hard indeed at the beginning of the time when they first came here to make their homes. But even long ago, there were many places deep in the thicket where a family or two could live."

"What I can't understand is how those loggers who want this land can manage to cut down trees and get them out of the Thicket," Ki said, frowning.

"They will learn as our people did, Ki," Fletache said. "I have heard our old men tell that when they saw a tree that was dead but had not yet fallen to the ground, a number of them went to cut it down so that they would have wood for their cooking-fires. They felled the tree and chopped off its branches and cut the trunk into short pieces to carry away."

"That won't satisfy the loggers, will it?" Jessie asked. "They'll want to get the tree trunks out whole."

"That is what I came to understand after I had given this thing some thought," Fletache replied. "And at night when they had come back from exploring the Thicket, I began to go close to the camp they had made at the edge and listen to them. And I heard them talking of ways to get the tree trunks out."

"Then they did figure out a way?" Jessie asked.

"A bad way, Jessie. They plan to cut the bushes and put them down to make roads that their ox teams can go over. Then they will chop off the branches of the trees they have cut down and make what they call skids to hold the tree trunks so that ox-teams can drag them to the bayou. Then they will float the tree trunks down to Galveston Bay and load them on ships."

"But if they did that, and kept cutting the timber over a very long period of time, they'd destroy the entire Big Thicket!" Jessie exclaimed.

"Yes. This I thought of, too." Fletache nodded. "That is when I decided to go and ask your father to help me."

"I don't know that I can be as much help as he could've been," Jessie said, "but Ki and I will both do our best."

"First we must get to a safe place," Fletache told her. "I do not think that any of the men who wish to cut the trees are here now. I have watched carefully while we were on the way, but I saw no sign of them, or of any camp they have made."

"If any of them are around, they're likely to be hiding a little way deeper in the Thicket," Jessie said thoughtfully. "You told us the way we came here, up the stream to this little lake, was the quickest and easiest way to get here, so if we used it, they must have—"

She broke off as a rifle shot cracked from somewhere in the dense brush that surrounded them and a bullet splashed into the marshy bog that still separated the boat from the shore. It was short of the boat by several feet, but the shot which followed almost at once landed in the mucky water close enough to send a shower of brown drops spattering over the dugout.

"You and Ki lie down in the bottom, Jessie," Fletache said quickly. "I will pole us back to the river and then we will go further upstream to another creek that I know about."

Jessie was too busy to obey the Tonkawa's command. She'd already picked up her Winchester, which at the beginning of their trip in the dugout she'd placed atop the heap of luggage that filled the craft's center. While Fletache freed the push-pole and stood up to dig it into the soft streambed, she was levering a shell into the rifle's chamber. Her eyes were searching the dense undergrowth when she heard a small, muted splash behind her as the Tonkawa thrust the pole to push the dugout back into the slowly moving current of the creek.

A third shot from the dense brush sent a bullet into the thick, sturdy gunwale of the boat, and the rifle slug buried itself harmlessly in the solid wooden stern of the long, narrow craft. Jessie had been watching the area beyond the creek mouth, where the sniper was hidden in the sunless shadows and dense vegetation. Her keen eyes bored into the heavy growth and she caught a glimpse of muzzle flash from the hidden sniper's rifle, followed by the dissipating wisp of powder smoke that followed.

Aiming with greater care now, shifting the muzzle of her rifle to bracket the area where she'd seen the quickly vanished thread of smoke, she let off the five shells that remained in the Winchester's magazine. Although she warned herself that the distant cry of pain she was sure she heard might have been wind in the treetops or nothing more than her imagination, Jessie was sure that at least one of her shots had found a target.

She kept her eyes fixed on the area while Fletache poled the unwieldy dugout backward out of the little creek until they'd reached the river's sullen, greenish current. No more shots came from the concealing growth, and Jessie saw no further signs of motion.

"I can't be sure, but I think I put one rifle slug into whoever that was shooting at us," she said to Ki and Fletache as the dugout entered a wide sweeping curve that quickly hid it from whoever had been sniping. "I don't suppose we'll ever know, though."

"Perhaps not," Fletache agreed. His forehead was wrinkled and he spoke slowly and thoughtfully, without taking his eyes off the creek's meandering course. "The shots may have been fired by some outlaw hiding in the Thicket. But it may have been one of the Old People. There were many of them when we Tonkawas came here to make our homes."

"Old People?" Jessie asked. "Who are they?"

"Our oldest men said they were what few people remain from the Alabamu and the Coushatta. Their tribes were driven from east of the Mississippi River before your states fought their war with the British. I am sure that in safe places, deep in the Thicket, there may be a few of their descendants left."

"I'd say that about all we can be sure of is that anyone we might meet from here on out isn't necessarily going to be a friend," Ki observed. "Especially if he happens to be nursing a fresh bullet wound."

As though to underscore what Ki had just said, another gunshot cracked from the underbrush along the riverbank. The bullet hit the river's surface with a high-pitched hissing screech, cut a short, shallow furrow in the water and rose from its surface just as it reached the dugout to land with a thunk in its side.

"Get down!" Jessie called as her eyes searched the shore for telltale powder smoke. "That sniper's following us along the bank!"

She obeyed her own command by dropping to the bottom of the dugout, and as she stretched out and looked back, she saw that Ki had taken cover between the heap of luggage and supplies. The only response Fletache had made to her warning was to kneel in the stern of the boat where the luggage and supply boxes formed a partial shield. He'd slid his hands down the push-pole and was still propelling the dugout back toward the river.

Jessie's first thought was that Fletache should not allow himself to become a target at her expense. She straightened up, shouldering her rifle as she moved, and let off two random shots at the screening brush. No replying shot came from the dense tangle of vegetation on the shore.

Reaching into her belt pouch for fresh shells to refill the Winchester's magazine, Jessie lowered the rifle's muzzle to rest on the thwart beside her while she slid the shells into the loading port. Whoever was sniping at them was obviously watching closely, for the hidden shootist grasped the opportunity Jessie had given him. Another shot rang out from the brush and the slug cut through the air between Jessie and Fletache.

Looking toward shore as she slid the last of the cartridges into the rifle, Jessie glimpsed a thin, dissipating wisp of muzzle smoke, a mere gray shadow drifting from shore across the surface of the water. Without moving her eyes away from the fast vanishing thread of muzzle smoke, again she bracketed the area from which the shots had come.

This time she could see the undergrowth moving as the sniper changed his position. The cover that concealed the hidden rifleman was a thick growth of weeds and grasses and a few tall, thin-stemmed flowers, all rooted in the unstable soil that gleamed wetly between the water's edge and the trees.

"Did you see the brush moving back from the shore there, Ki?" she asked.

"Yes. And I agree with you. I will go to the right and you to the left, and we'll corner him between us."

Chapter 6

Jessie rose to a crouch and started to step out of the dugout. She stopped short when Fletache called sharply, "No, Jessie! There are alligators bigger than men in this water!"

Jessie pulled her foot back quickly. Then she asked, "How are we going to get to shore, then?"

"We can't. Not here. There will be a place just ahead where we can step safely from the boat onto the shore. Lie in the bottom of the boat while I pole us to it, then we can go hunt down the man shooting at us!"

Jessie made an instant decision. She laid the Winchester aside and drew her Colt, knowing that the high-velocity slug from the rifle could be deflected by even a flower stem, while the heavier and slower moving hunk of lead from the revolver would plow through the thin-stemmed growth at the water's edge.

Her eyes fixed on the undergrowth, she waited until she saw another movement of the ground over, and bracketed the area of shaking vegetation with three quick shots from the Colt. Once again there was movement in the brush, but whoever or whatever was the cause remained hidden.

Jessie kept her attention focused on the shoreline at the point where the quivering tips of the high-screening growth indicated the location of the sniper who'd been firing at them. She was groping in her ammunition pouch for fresh shells when the dugout lurched and rocked and she heard a splash behind her. Turning, she saw Ki standing in the knee-deep water beside the boat. He took a step toward the shore, and suddenly dropped until his hips were at the surface. Still he kept pushing forward, fighting the sluggish current and the deep muck on the bottom that kept him from moving with his usual speed.

"No, Ki!" Jessie exclaimed. "You can't wade fast enough!"

As though to underline Jessie's warning, the sniper fired again, the slug from his rifle splashing into the murky water only an inch from Ki's body. Ki dropped flat, sending up a sheet of the dark water. He began trying to swim, but the mucky bottom refused to release him. At last he kicked free and started moving slowly in a half-submerged alligatorlike crawl toward the bank.

Jessie reached for her rifle, remembered that its magazine was empty, and raised her Colt to trigger off its last two shells. A loud yell of pain from the undergrowth told her that at last she'd fired an effective shot, for no report came from the hidden sniper's rifle in response to her bullet.

"Maybe I've put our sniper out of commission, Ki!" she called. "Now, turn around and get back in the boat so that we can move away from here!"

His slow movements showing his reluctance to retreat, Ki turned in the water and struggled back. His progress was slow, with the soupy bottom sucking at his feet, but at last he reached the dugout and levered himself over its low gunwale.

Fletache had been holding the clumsy craft in place against the creek's sluggish current. "That was a foolish thing you did, Ki," he said. His voice held no anger, but it was stern, and his face was drawn into a worried frown. He went on, "I will ask one thing of you and Jessie now. Do not go into water or onto any places where the earth underfoot is wet until I tell you it is safe."

"Fletache's right, Ki," Jessie agreed. "I'll do what he says, and so must you."

Ki's expression did not change from its usual impassiveness as he nodded and said, "You're right, of course. I promise you that I will not do such a foolish thing again."

Now, with Ki back on board, Fletache resumed his poling. There was still no sign of activity from the rifleman who'd been sniping at them from the shore.

"My guess is that the gang after that timber left somebody to watch the area," Jessie said as they moved slowly downstream. "And perhaps to scout around as well."

"That is possible, Jessie." Fletache nodded. "But there are also many here in the swamp who have found the Thicket a good place to hide from the lawmen who are looking for them. They shoot at any stranger who comes close."

"And you said there were some of the old tribes who came here from the east," Ki put in, his voice thoughtful. "I don't suppose they welcome visitors in a very friendly way."

"There are not many of them, Ki. I have seen only two or three of the Old People myself, and that was long before I had grown to manhood. In the last few years I have not seen any."

They'd reached the mouth of the creek by now, and the big Tonkawa fell silent as he put aside the push-pole and picked up the oar. Hunkering down in the stern, he maneuvered the dugout through the swirling eddies that roiled the surface where the creek flowed into the river, and he began paddling harder as the dugout encountered the heavier current of the larger stream.

Jessie busied herself with her weapons after they entered the river. She thumbed shells into the Winchester's magazine and laid the weapon at her feet, then put fresh loads into the Colt's cylinder before restoring it to its holster.

While she was working, Ki removed his *shuriken* from his vest pocket. He took out each of the shining star-shaped blades in turn and wiped them carefully, then laid them in neat rows on the load to dry. After he'd stripped off his sopping jacket and emptied its capacious pockets he spread it out beside the throwing-blades.

While Jessie and Ki were tending to their weapons, Fletache guided the dugout into the mouth of another creek less than a quarter of a mile from the one they'd left. This was a smaller stream, but a deeper one, and from the increase in Fletache's exertions with the oar, Jessie could tell that the current was much heavier.

Slowly, the dugout moved upstream against the constant tug of the water's sluggish flow. The day was ending now, and the massed vegetation that rose from the shore seemed to swallow the fading twilight. There was barely enough of a glow in the sky to make out the shoreline when Fletache headed the dugout to the bank. He stopped the clumsy craft before it reached the land, laying the oar aside and picking up the push-pole. Driving the pole into the river bottom he looped the dugout's bowline around the sturdy wooden shaft.

"We must sleep in the boat tonight," he announced. "This is a part of the Thicket that is very dangerous in the dark. Men fleeing from the law come to it, and they have not learned to understand its night noises. They often shoot at sounds even when they cannot see what caused them. Tomorrow, we will go up the other creek until we reach a place where there is another trail that we can follow to my cabin."

"I don't know which is worse," Jessie remarked as she tried to swallow a bite of the hard ship's bread they'd brought along with their small stock of emergency rations, "biting off a chunk of this bread or trying to chew it."

"It's better than being hungry," Ki replied. He'd been looking at the sky, which was beginning to gray with dawn light. "But not by very much, no matter how you take it."

"We have not had a restful night," Fletache said. "But there is a cave I know of along the trail where we can stop and sleep for a while."

"How long will it take us to get there?" Jessie asked.

"Not as long as the trail will seem," the Tonkawa said, a smile on his face. "First we must go up this creek to the smaller creek which will take us to the trail, then it is but a short distance to the cave. We can rest there, and still reach my cabin before dark."

As he spoke, Fletache was untying the rope that secured the dugout to the push-pole. He headed into the current, and the dugout began moving slowly into the creek.

Instead of the marshland they'd encountered in the larger creek they'd entered first, the banks of this stream wound between tall trees. Fletache was forced to pole the dugout more slowly now as the creek narrowed and its current grew stronger. As they'd progressed, the banks had begun to shelve higher and wind through the tangled forest in sharper and more frequent turns as they moved upstream.

With her weapons attended to, Jessie could pay more

attention to their surroundings. She found that she could put names to only a few of the trees that grew in clusters along the creek and on the higher land away from it. She was familiar with pines from her own experience with the Starbuck timberlands in the west, but the pines she saw now grew taller and spindlier, and for every kind of tree that was familiar to her there were three varieties which she was looking at for the first time.

She could identify the small stands of oaks and maple and ash and hickory and elm mixed in with the pines, because she'd learned of them during her New England schooling. After Fletache had identified the cypresses for her, Jessie had no trouble spotting them, because of their massive tapered trunks that rose twenty or thirty feet into the air with a thin conical taper before the first branches appeared. Still, there were other varieties that she could not name growing in small clusters here and there.

While they traveled the last vestiges of darkness were being rolled back by the bright sky, filled now with its sunrise glow. The treetops were silhouetted now as dark lines against the blue sky. Here the trees grew down to the water's edge, with only a thin line of river reeds and high, sparse-branched shrubs between them and the bank.

When Fletache finally headed the dugout to shore and leaped out to secure it to a thick-limbed bush with only tufts of leaves at the tips of its branches, Jessie and Ki stood up and began to stretch before stepping to shore.

"It's no wonder the timber cutters want this land," Jessie said to Fletache. "I've never seen such a variety of trees in such a small space before."

"Without the trees, the land is nothing," he replied. "And even here in the Thicket, where the earth is rich and soft and there is never any lack of water, most trees do not grow quickly."

"I can see why you want to keep the loggers out," Ki said. "Not only because—"

He broke off suddenly and dived toward the center of the dugout, where his *shuriken* still lay in their neat array on the craft's load. He picked up one of the glittering blades and was cocking his arm back to send it spinning through the air when a sheepish grin formed on his face and he lowered his poised forearm slowly.

Jessie's eyes had followed Ki's, and her hand was dropping to the butt of her Colt when she stopped it in midair.

While they were still staring at the strange object which had triggered their defensive moves, Fletache spoke.

"I should have warned you," he said. "But it is good for me to know that my warning sign still does what I intended it to do."

Neither Jessie nor Ki spoke at once. They stepped to shore to join Fletache, their eyes still fixed on the rain-bleached human skeleton that was dangling by a rope from the lowest branch of a towering pine tree that grew with its roots at the water's edge. The white bones swayed gently in the light breeze at the end of a hangman's knot in the rope that held it high above the ground.

"I know what I'm looking at," Jessie said after gazing at the skeletal remains for a silent moment. "But what on earth is that skeleton doing there?"

"I am sorry, Jessie," Fletache apologized. "But I am so used to seeing it that I forgot to warn you and Ki not to be alarmed when we reached it."

Ki put in quickly, "I'm as curious as Jessie is, Fletache. They look like the bones of a man who was hanged on that tree limb, but I know they can't possibly be."

"Why do you say that?" the Tonkawa asked.

"Because the bones are so weather-bleached," Ki replied promptly. "All the sinews between the joints in that skeleton would've rotted away if it had been hanging there long enough for the bones to be as white as they are. And when the sinews rot away, the bones in a skeleton fall apart."

"You think faster than most men, Ki." Fletache smiled. "But you are right. I have spent many hours working on that skeleton to keep all its bones together."

"And my guess is that you find it's useful as a warning sign to keep intruders away," Jessie said.

"Of course," Fletache agreed. "But the skeleton is real, Jessie. Look at the tree trunk if you would like to read the story of how it came to be there."

Jessie and Ki started toward the trunk of the soaring pine. As they got closer to the skeleton they saw that strips of rawhide had been carefully inserted into holes drilled through the bones above and below each joint and knotted to keep the skeletal form intact. They also saw that a section of the bark on the tree's trunk had been cut away, and lines that formed a picture-story were incised into the wood itself.

At a distance the lines had seemed no more than rough scratchings, but when Jessie and Ki reached the pine's massive trunk, the seemingly aimless marks took shape into pictures that told their own story.

Though the depiction was crude, it was easily understood. The carving was in two sections, one above the other. The upper section showed a number of horned steers being driven by a horseman wearing a bandana mask over the lower part of his face. Below it the second picture showed the masked man dangling from the limb of a tree, just as the skeleton was now dangling above Jessie and Ki and Fletache.

"A cattle rustler and his fate!" Jessie exclaimed. "And my guess is that these carvings were made by one of the men who chased the rustler and hanged him!"

"That's what I took it to be, just as you do," Fletache agreed. "When we Tonkawas were first sent here by Sam Houston, they found the rustler's corpse hanging here. Our old men are all dead now, but they were young warriors then. They have told me of seeing it."

"And they just let it hang?" Jessie asked.

"Of course. The carving on the tree trunk was fresh, too, at the time they came here. Later, when the man's body began to decompose and fall apart, our medicine men put the bones back together and hung the skeleton where it was then, just as it is now. I don't suppose it kept away any of the outlaws who hid in the Big Thicket then, just as they still do today, but the few cattle our people brought with them when they came here were never bothered."

"Gruesome, but effective," Ki remarked. "Do you have any more surprises like this waiting for us ahead, Fletache?"

"No," the Tonkawa answered, shaking his head. "None like this one. But I'm sure you'll be surprised by other things that we will see on our way to my home."

"How far is it?" Jessie asked.

"If we are to stop and sleep at the cave I told you of, we will not reach it today," Fletache told her. "That is why I started up the other creek where we had to turn back after the sniper shot at us; we would have had a much shorter distance to go. But it is better that we start rested, now that we must travel so much further."

"We can't take the boat any further, then?" Ki frowned.

Fletache shook his head. "This creek runs very shallow just a few hundred yards ahead, where it splits into two streams, so we must leave the boat here."

"Then if we've got such a long way to go, we'd better get started," Jessie suggested. "We've already lost a lot of time."

Working as smoothly as if they'd been traveling together for many weeks, they divided the load from the dugout between them. Fletache shouldered the heaviest bundles and took the lead, with Jessie behind him. She was lightly laden, a single small pack on her shoulders, her arms free to carry her Winchester and use it if the need arose. Ki brought up the rear, his back supporting a number of small bundles lashed together.

Fletache started up the long slope that led from the marked pine into a wall of brush. Even from a short distance away the wall of trees had seemed impenetrable, but before he reached the massive tangles of vari-hued green that rose in front of them, he slanted to one side and led them toward the brush.

A dozen steps took them to a break in the dense undergrowth. The narrow gap in the high, brushy barrier became a tunnel, with vines lining its sides, climbing the bushes, then snaking across gaps to the tree trunks and arching into the limbs of the trees that grew thickly as far as they could see. On all sides of the faint trail that meandered through the wild growth there were tall, nodding stalks of swamp buttercups mixed with the sturdier stems of dogwood and azaleas and lower-growing purple and yellow iris.

Ferns shot up everywhere, some of their fronded thick-clustered growth as tall as the heads of the trio making their way along the faint bare thread of foot-beaten earth that formed the trail. Tall trunks of loblolly pines rose above the undergrowth to mingle their branches with outspread limbs of longleaf pines and wide-spreading umbrella-shaped oak and hickory trees. In the low areas between hillocks the tapering thick-branched trunks of high-rising cypress trees were reflected on the glinting mirror-smooth surface of shallow ponds where they were rooted.

"I've never seen anything like this before," Jessie turned to remark to Ki as they followed the giant Tonkawa. Both she and Ki were keeping close behind Fletache as he strode confidently ahead along the barely-visible trail, pushing aside the branches of the whipping brush. She went on, "I thought I'd seen just about everything there is to see in Texas, and I've heard a little bit about the Big Thicket, but I never dreamed it was like this."

"I'm learning something new, too," Ki replied. "But I've already decided one thing."

"What's that?" Jessie asked.

"I would never want to run a herd of cattle in a place like this."

"They certainly wouldn't be able to stray very far."

"No. But think how long it'd take to find a stray in all the undergrowth."

"I'd rather not," Jessie replied. "It's hard enough to find strays on the open prairie, but in a place like this you could look for them forever and never see one if it was ten steps away from you."

"It is a good place to hide, though," Fletache put in. "If it had not been for the Thicket, all of my people would have been killed by our tribal enemies long before my mother bore me. But we had—"

Fletache's words were interrupted by a shot and the high-pitched whine of a rifle bullet. The slug was too high to find a ground target. It passed over their heads and thunked into the trunk of one of the low-branching pin-oaks in the stand they were passing through.

"Hurry!" the big Tonkawa urged as he motioned for Jessie and Ki to follow him. "If we don't move quickly, we will be trapped here! The man who was shooting at us in the boat must know the Thicket as well as I do. He has gone through the woods to this creek, trying to cut us off!"

★

Chapter 7

Fletache was stepping away from the trail as he spoke, his big arms parting the tree limbs that hung low along the faint winding trail through the oak thicket. Another shot sounded from the rifle of the still invisible sniper. The bullet that followed the report whistled with an angry whine above their heads, then cut through the low-hanging branches and sped on past them to sing its way through the brush.

Jessie and Ki wasted no time following Fletache into the dense underbrush. They saw no trail, but it was obvious to him that the Tonkawa knew exactly where he was going. Pushing aside the low-hanging tree branches that tangled with the shrubs and brush below them, he opened a path for them as they plunged into the wild growth.

In such an alien terrain it was impossible for anyone to move carefully. On almost every tree the vines shot up from the soft, moist earth. Their growth from the ground was in the form of root-stems as large as Jessie's wrist, and after coiling up the bole of a tree these root-stems expanded their reach along its lowest branches in dozens of finger-sized tendrils.

Scores of wild shoots, some toothpick-tiny, others the diameter of matchsticks, sprouted from the tendrils to a length of ten or fifteen feet. These attached themselves in springy coils around the tree branches or recircled almost as tightly as metal springs around the parent root, and equally often dangled loosely from the parent stem to hang as thick as a curtain between the limbs of adjoining trees.

Even Fletache, who had grown to manhood in the Big Thicket, could not have made a silent passage through the tangled and intertwined vines; nor did he try. His big hands grasped the small stems and he pulled them away, tearing them from the parent plant, to form a narrow slit through which the three could pass. Progress was slow, and noisy. They had to thresh their feet to kick them free of the vines that had reached the earth and run along it like cords, ready to trip anyone who made a careless step.

"Aren't we making a lot of noise?" Jessie asked Fletache after they'd covered forty or fifty feet from the dugout.

"Yes. But whoever is shooting at us must know the Thicket as well as I do," Fletache replied. "He understands that a gun is useless in places such as this. Any bullet he might fire would be deflected only a few feet from where he stands."

"What do you think he'll do, then?" she pressed.

"He must do one of only two things," the Tonkawa said. "He can try to find us by the noise we are making, and shoot at close range, or he can wait until we stop, and then try. But by the time he decides, we will be in a safe place."

"What do you call a safe place?" Ki asked.

"We are near the cave I have spoken of. It is an old bear's den, but it has not been used by bears for many years. It is only a short distance ahead, and once we get to it we will be safe. If the man who was shooting at us knows the Thicket as well as I think he must, he will either try to follow us by the noise we are making, or he will wait quietly until we take cover, and track us to our hiding place by the vines and bushes we have torn."

"I see." Jessie frowned thoughtfully. "Well, let's go on to your bear's den, Fletache. If he follows our trail and finds us, at least we'll be ready to shoot first."

A quarter of an hour spent fighting their way through the tangle had brought Jessie, Ki, and Fletache to a small clearing, a burned-over area that covered two or three acres of a rounded rise. Hip-high stumps stood thick over the little hump, their charred pointed tops giving evidence that the clear area had once been part of a dense stand of tall trees. The clearing extended from the tangle of the living woods to the rough, gray rim of a stone outcrop that arced over a third of one edge and covered it completely. On the remaining portion the stumps rose from a thick cover of vines and creepers that covered the ground. In several places at the highest point of the rise, humped tops of man-tall boulders rose above the green growth.

"How on earth could there be a forest fire in a place as wet as this?" Jessie asked as she and Ki followed Fletache up the slope to its boulder-strewn top.

"As my people would say, fire from the sky struck here," the Tonkawa replied. "There are other open spaces like this in the Thicket where high pine trees once grew. Not all of them are as big, and none of the others have stones in them."

"I suppose the fires were caused by lightning bolts?"

"Pines grow taller than the other trees here, Jessie,"

Fletache said. "They pull down the flashes that leap to earth from the heavens."

"Of course." Jessie nodded. "Like lightning rods."

Pointing to the overhanging rock formation, Ki asked, "I don't suppose we can see it yet, but I imagine the old bear den you mentioned is under that big rock shelf?"

"Yes, Ki. We go to that side—" Fletache broke off to raise his arm and point to the right-hand side of the granite dome—"and the entrance is just beyond the tallest stump."

"Let's get there and take cover, then," Jessie suggested. "After traveling through all that thick undergrowth we've been fighting since we left the boat, I'm about ready to get to a place where we can sleep and be safe at the same time."

Refreshed by their pause, brief though it had been, they angled across the burned-over area toward the edge of the granite dome. Though the vines that crept over so much of the ground caught their feet occasionally, they were nothing but a minor nuisance compared to the dense undergrowth they'd been battling since leaving the dugout.

They reached the edge of the massive stone dome and followed Fletache as he led them at a sharp angle toward its low, narrow face. After they'd gone only a few paces they could see the beginning of the opening he'd described so sketchily. The face of the dome-shaped granite slab was buried in the earth at the point where they'd first seen it. Now they observed a crack beginning to show between rock and earth. Suddenly the crack became a black gap, then a yawning hole. Soon they could see the face of the rock outcrop in its entirety. Between the rim of the outcrop and the soft ground there was a midnight-black oval gap through which a tall man could walk without stooping.

"I don't suppose by any chance a bear could still be inside?" Jessie asked.

"Not at this season," the Tonkawa said. "And as I have told you, the cave hasn't been used by a bear for many years."

Ki started toward the yawning black gap. From a distance the entrance to the cavern had looked like an oversized mouth opened wide, and it still gave that impression now that they were closer. The rock shelf curved upward in a gentle arc which was repeated in reverse by the ground below it.

Beyond the humped top of the massive stone formation, the sun had now cleared the treetops. It was still low enough for its rays to reach Ki's eyes. He blinked and was bringing up his arm to shield his face when he caught a glimpse of the ghost of a motion from the blackness beneath the overhanging rock.

Ki reacted with the swiftest move of which his sharply honed reflexes were capable. In a series of lightninglike moves he shoved Jessie away from him on one side, then circled in his steps to push Fletache away on the other. Then he dropped flat himself just as a gun roared and a streak of red muzzle-blast spurted from the darkness of the opening ahead.

Ki's dive ended in the fraction of a second before the whistling slug from the rifle fired in the cave passed close enough for him to feel the breath of air disturbed by its passage. As he hit the ground he was reaching into his vest pocket for a *shuriken*. Behind him he heard Jessie's Colt bark, and the crack of the revolver was followed by a dull metallic scraping as the bullet met the inner wall of the cavern.

"It's the sniper who was shooting at us back along the creek!" Jessie said. "He must have holed up to wait for us!"

"He knew of the bear den, too," Fletache agreed. "But

we can circle around it and go on. It will mean giving up our rest, but then we will—"

"No!" Ki broke in. "Let's get that sniping devil out of our way for good. I can get to that cave with *ninjitsu*. He won't be able to stop me."

"But there is only bare ground between us and the cave!" Fletache objected. "You cannot—"

"Yes, he can," Jessie interrupted. "And I—"

She broke off as a man's voice called from the cavern's darkness, "Let up shooting! I wasn't meaning to start no fight or hurt you folks or Fletache! I didn't spot him right off! I figured you was some of them damn timber pirates!"

"It's all right," Fletache said quickly. "I know who it is now. His name is Barkey. He lives here in the Thicket; he is not one of the timber looters."

"That's sure gospel truth, Fletache!" the man in the cave called. "I never did have no fuss with you or your folks. I'll come on out right now if you and your friends won't hold my fool mistake agin me."

Fletache looked questioningly at Jessie. She said, "If you know him and think it's all right for him to come out, Ki and I certainly won't object."

Raising his voice a bit, the Tonkawa called, "Come on out, Jeff! None of us has any quarrel with you, either."

A moment or two passed before the man in the cave emerged. He was a rawboned, rangy individual who seemed just a bit larger than life. It had been necessary for him to bend forward to get out of the opening of the cave.

His full brown beard started high on his cheekbones, making his pale blue eyes appear as slits between the beard's first growth and his bushy eyebrows. It fanned out from his cheeks to cover the better part of his chest, and ended in a ragged line that was almost level with his expansive waist.

He was wearing a battered black felt hat that had several small jagged holes in its crown, and in a number of places the oval line of its wide brim was broken by torn slits and small, raggedly shredded indentations, as though the hat had been chewed by small animals. The jacket he wore had been cobbled together from a number of rabbit skins. Its sleeves fell six inches short of covering his wrists. Faded denim miner's jeans and a pair of deerskin moccasins completed his wardrobe.

In addition to the ancient short-barreled Maynard carbine which he gripped by the stock's throat in one massive hand, he was armed with an Old Model Colt Navy revolver which he wore in a rawhide holster that dangled from the right-hand side of a wide leather belt low on his hips. The grip of what Jessie took to be a small bowie knife was sticking out of its sheath on the belt's opposite side.

Stopping just outside the cave's mouth, the newcomer looked at Jessie and Ki for a moment, then said to Fletache, "I'm real sorry about shooting at your friends here. Like I said, I didn't see you right off, and I didn't make out that one of 'em was a lady. When I heerd you coming, I taken you for that blasted timber pirate I was following. He cut across my track while I was heading for the river before daybreak, then I lost him. I heard you folks coming before I seen you, so I dived into the cave to watch and see what you was doing."

"Have the timber cutters been moving around a lot lately?" Fletache asked.

"Not as much as they was, Fletache," the newcomer replied. "When I run across that fellow's tracks this morning, I figured they'd begun prowling again and thought I'd give 'em something else to think about."

Nodding, the Tonkawa turned to Jessie and Ki. "This is Jefferson Barkey. He is one of us who make our home in the Big Thicket. Jeff, this is Miss Jessica Starbuck and her friend's name is Ki. I went seeking Miss Starbuck's father, who many years ago promised to help me if I needed him. He made the promise in return for a small favor I had done him. Her father is dead now, but Miss Starbuck has honored his promise and come here in his place."

Barkey nodded. "I got the message you left with my old woman, but she didn't tell me no names." He turned to Jessie and went on, "I'm right glad to see you, ma'am, and I sure hope you brought a lot of men with you, because them timber pirates is dead set on tearing down what me and Fletache and lots of other folks call our home."

"Please don't be disappointed when I tell you that Ki and I didn't bring anyone with us," Jessie said. "But we'll do our best to keep your homes from being destroyed."

"Well, damn my buttons if you..." Barkey exclaimed. He stopped and shook his head, then went on, "'Scuse me, Miss Starbuck. I forget to watch my damn tongue...." Again he halted, then grinned sheepishly and said, "Well, you know a man's got to cuss now and again, so jist take the will for the deed. But what I was trying to git around to, there's a bunch of them tree butchers just waiting out at the edge of the Thicket to start cutting. How can you and this little fellow do anything to stop 'em?"

"Ask me that after I've found out more about the situation here," Jessie suggested. "But it might ease your worries to know that we have stopped them for a while."

"Now, how in—how in tunket did you do that?" Barkey frowned. "From the looks of it, you and your man Ki jest got here."

"They did," Fletache said quickly. "But Jessie knows how to use the law, Jeff. Right this minute, she's got lawyers back in San Antonio and Houston working to stop the timber cutters."

"That's right good news," the swampman said. He turned to Jessie and went on, "You figure you can hold 'em off, then?"

"There's a chance, yes," Jessie answered. "But there's an equally good chance that we might have to use a few bullets before it's all finished."

"I'm your man, whichever way it goes," Barkey said. "Now, is there something I can do to help you right off?"

"Yes, there is," the Tonkawa said promptly. "Jessie needs to rest; we had little sound sleep last night. While she and Ki stay here, you can go back with me to the boat to help unload the gear we've brought along and then help us carry it to my cabin."

"They're figuring to stay here in the Thicket?" the swampman asked, his jaw dropping.

"We certainly are," Jessie assured him. "As long as it takes to get rid of the timber cutters."

"Well, if I know us Thicket folks, you and your friend will sure be welcome, little lady," Barkey told her.

"I'm glad to hear you say that, Jeff," Fletache said. "I was a bit worried that some of our friends here in the Thicket might not welcome outsiders."

"Not this time, Fletache," Barkey replied. "I been doing some talking around with our friends, and doing some listening, too. There's plenty of us Thicketers that's fretting pretty bad because we've mostly been here so long we've just about forgot what it's like outside. A lot of us don't take so good to things we ain't used to."

Ki broke in to say, "This is something we can talk about later. Jessie needs to rest. Fletache, why don't we let her stay here and nap while I go back to the creek to help you bring our gear and provisions up here?"

"Don't you think you should stay with Jessie, to keep an eye open while she sleeps?" Fletache asked.

"Nonsense!" Jessie broke in before Ki could reply. "I'll be quite all right alone, hidden in that cave."

"I'm sure you will, or I wouldn't've offered to go," Ki said. "The boat's not all that far away. We'll only be gone an hour or so."

"We should start at once, then," Fletache suggested. "We still have a long walk to reach my cabin."

After she'd watched the men leave to go to the dugout, Jessie turned back to the gaping cave-mouth that yawned black across the little clearing. The opening was high enough at its center for her to walk inside without stooping. She stepped into the blackness and stopped to let her vision adjust to the darkness. Bit by bit, the interior became visible. Now Jessie could see that the cavern was shaped like a bubble, its interior roofed with rock, its earthen floor clean and dry. For a few moments she searched the dimness, trying to select a place to lie down, but each square foot of the floor was so like every other that she quickly realized that there was no point in trying to make a choice.

Her eyes seemed to blur as the interior of the cavern became more readily visible, and Jessie realized that the fast-moving events of the past few days, the constant travel and the sleeplessness of the previous night had tired her a great deal more than she'd realized. She was still standing near the center of the big semi-underground chamber. She laid down her rifle and stretched out beside it, crooking her arm to form a headrest. Within a very few moments she was caught by the deep sleep that comes with exhaustion.

An evil-smelling hand closing tightly over Jessie's mouth and chin brought her awake with a start. Her eyes flew open and she saw the face of a strange man only a few inches above her own. Her muscles tensed instinctively as she tried to move, only to realize that other hands were holding her wrists immobile and pinning her booted feet to the ground.

She saw the second man then for the first time when she looked down. Returning her gaze to the grimy, unshaven face of the man crouched beside her shoulders, Jessie tried to speak, but his hands pressed to her face reduced her words to nothing but a series of unintelligible muffled noises confined to her throat. She struggled with all her considerable strength, but the hands retained their grips.

"Now, jest get quiet," the man leaning over her head said. "You ain't going to break away from me and Caleb. We've took dames like you before now. We c'n handle you, all right."

"Damn right we can, Snatcher!" The man holding Jessie's feet chuckled. "But it's been a long time since we run into one that's as young and purty as this one."

"Yep," the man addressed as Snatcher agreed. "I told you what she looked like when I come to git you to help me."

Jessie tried to speak, but Snatcher had not relaxed his grip on her mouth and chin. All she could utter was an unintelligible gargling deep in her throat. Realizing the uselessness of continuing to try to speak, she lay quietly.

"Well, now we got her, we best haul her outta here fast," Caleb said. "Them fellows that was in the boat with her's not likely to be gone much longer. I don't aim to let them get anyplace close to us."

"Now, that's real true," Snatcher replied. "Go ahead and tie up her feet. I'll keep hold of her mouth. If she gits to kicking too bad for you to handle 'em, I'll just cut off her air till she goes under."

"Hell, no! Don't try that again! I don't want for you to kill her, like you done the last one! Not yet, anyways."

While her captors had been discussing their next moves, Jessie's mind had worked at top speed. It was obvious that the two men were plug-uglies hired by the timber pirates who were planning to take the trees out of the Big Thicket. That they had a camp of some sort close by was also obvious. Jessie made a quick decision.

Certain that the combined skills of Ki and Fletache and Jeff Barkey would quickly bring about her release, she decided to offer no more resistance. She formed a stifled moan deep in her throat, closed her eyes, and let her muscles go limp.

Chapter 8

"Damn it, do what I told you to, Snatcher!" Jessie heard Caleb say. "Ain't you got no sense at all?"

"Don't get so riled up!" Snatcher growled. "I know what I'm doing! All I done is put her to sleep for a little while, so she won't be fighting us when we start to carry her."

"All right." Caleb's voice was grudging. "But grab that pistol outta her holster before she comes to. I reckon if she's carrying it she might have a pretty good idee how to use it."

Jessie felt Snatcher's rough hands on her as he moved her in order to slide out her revolver. Then she heard him say, "Nice gun—maybe the best one I ever seen. She ain't going to be needing it no more, so I reckon I'll just keep it. It's a good sight better'n this old Navy Colt I'm packing now."

"Well, put the damn gun away till later!" Caleb snapped. "You can look at all you feel like later on. You better take off that bandana you got around your neck and lash her damn jaws closed right now. And don't strangle her like you did the last one! This one looks too good to miss out on!"

Jessie continued to feign unconsciousness while Snatcher, holding her head, tied a foul-smelling bandana around her mouth. Then, not wanting to overplay her hand, she began to stir when Caleb pressed her shoulders to the ground while his companion started lashing her arms together. She was careful to hide her real strength, and made only token struggles against the outlaw who was wrapping rawhide thongs around her crossed wrists while Caleb held her shoulders in place.

She fought awkwardly against Snatcher by thrashing her arms and jerking her knees up in an effort to kick him while she twisted against his companion's pressure on her shoulders. Only once was Jessie forced to bring her full strength into play. When Snatcher closed his big horny hand around her wrists she wriggled them and turned them in his hand while she kicked and squirmed, to make sure that her wrists would be edge-to-edge instead of with their flat inner sides together while he tied them.

Aided by her kicking and squirming, Jessie managed to hold her wrists firmly pressed in the position she wanted them to be as Snatcher tightened and knotted the rawhide thongs he was using. Then, when he moved his attention to her ankles, Jessie gambled for the second time. Crossing her ankles, she brought up her knees and let them spread apart as though by accident, ignoring the sight she was creating by forcing her short knee-length riding skirt to slide up her soft white thighs.

As she'd hoped and expected, Snatcher could not take his eyes off the creamy skin of her inner thighs, which she'd bared by her move. Instead of forcing her legs straight and circling them from calf to ankle with his thongs, the outlaw kept watching her exposed thighs while he wrapped the bonds around her crossed ankles. He wound the leather strips in the cross of the X formed by her ankles instead of forcing her to hold her legs straight and winding the thongs around them.

"Well, damn you for a jackass, Snatcher!" Caleb snorted when he saw what his companion had done.

"What're you yowling about?" Snatcher asked, his eyes still fixed on Jessie's bared thighs.

"Why the hell didn't you pull her legs straight before you tied her feet?" Caleb shot back. "And then turn her over and tie her arms along her sides? If you'd've had gumption enough to tie her legs tight together, one of us could just sling her across our shoulder."

"Because she was bucking like a bronco all the time, dammit," Snatcher replied angrily. "You seen how she was doing! Anyhow, what difference does it make?"

"Even an idiot like you oughta know that! Now it's gonna take both of us to carry her!"

"What if it does?" Snatcher asked. "We're all three going to the same place."

"Sure. But them fellows that's gone down to the boat is going to get back here pretty soon. When they find the dame's gone they'll sure as sin take after us. How the hell are we gonna hold 'em off when both of us has got our hands full toting her? And how d'you think we're going to tote and carry our rifles, too?"

"Oh, stop your damn complaining, Caleb!" Snatcher's voice was almost a shout, his face flushed with anger. He went on quickly, "If you don't like the way I wrapped her up, I'll carry the dame by myself!"

Caleb was cooling down now. He was silent for a moment, then said, "Well, now that you've offered, I'll just take you up on it. Step over here, and I'll hoist her up for you."

"Just give me a hand getting her on my shoulder, that's all," Snatcher went on. Then he added, "A-course, if I carry her by myself, you'll have to tote both the rifles."

"Anything to get us started moving," Caleb sighed. "For all we know, them two fellows might be heading back from that boat right now."

"Don't waste no more time yattering at me, then. Let's pick up the dame and get moving!"

Still muttering angrily under his breath, Caleb moved to where Jessie lay bound and helped Snatcher hoist her crosswise atop his shoulders. With her arms and legs bound as they were, she made an ungainly load. Bending forward, Snatcher worked his torso up and down several times until he could balance Jessie on his back. Then he took an experimental forward step to be sure that he'd be able to walk.

"Well?" Caleb asked. "You gonna keep moving or not?"

"Give me a chance to get her set so's I can!" Snatcher shot back.

After a bit more time spent experimenting, Snatcher finally found that by holding Jessie's crossed wrists with one hand and extending his left arm to reach and grasp her legs he could still stand fairly erect and walk while carrying his burden.

"All right," he told his companion, "let's git going. The sooner we git away from here, the better off we'll be."

"You know, I've been thinking about what we oughta do," Caleb said as Snatcher bent forward to clear the overhang of the massive stone formation. "We'd be better off if we just holed up in here and pick off them two fellows that's with this dame when they come back."

"Damned if I'd wanta do that!" Snatcher replied. "They could keep us pinned down here forever and a day if we was to stay under this overhang! No, siree! We got her now, and I aim to keep her till I git tired of her. We ain't seen a woman here in the Thicket since we signed on with them timber cutters."

"You ain't the only one that's going to get a crack at her, you know," Caleb remarked as they started across the clearing toward its edge. "Once them other fellows find out what we got here, they're gonna be lining up and paying us good hard cash to take their whacks with her."

"From what I seen of her so far, she ain't going to like that one damn bit."

"What she likes or don't like won't matter a damn. We'll just tie her ankles to the bottom of the bed and her hands to the top. Then all a man needs to do is get on and ride till he's got his money's worth. Which he'll pay to you and me, a-course."

"Well, I won't object to that, either," Snatcher replied. "I hadn't thought about it till you come up with the idee, but a little extra money always comes in handy."

Jessie had been listening to her captors as they argued when Snatcher was tying her and while he struggled to get her balanced across his shoulders. With the gag in her mouth she'd been unable to respond, and all her efforts to rid herself of the foul-smelling and evil-tasting bandana had failed. So had her careful attempts to free herself from the thongs with which the pair had bound her.

Stifling her anger, Jessie forced herself to carry on her pose of semiconsciousness. After the first effort she'd made to free herself had shown her that more time would be needed to get rid of her bonds, she remained limp and motionless while Snatcher carried her slowly away from the cavern and started across the stump-studded clearing into the dense growth.

When they reached the tangled underbrush her captors separated. Caleb went ahead, picking the best path for

Snatcher to follow through the bush, which in most places grew almost chest-high. In areas where the ground was most heavily covered, it was necessary for Caleb to move only a half-step in front of his companion and part the thick bushes and hold them aside while Snatcher passed him and took a pace or two ahead. Then Caleb would push past Snatcher and Jessie and repeat the process while they advanced a few steps further. Neither of the pair had much to say as they made their slow progress along the trail, which was almost invisible in the tall and tangled undergrowth.

Neither of her captors had time to pay any attention to Jessie. They were too busy battling the brush. Now and then a ground-hugging root or sagging lower branch entangled Snatcher's feet, and he'd lurch forward, while Jessie tensed herself for the headlong fall which seemed inevitable. In spite of his ill-balanced load, the outlaw always managed to avoid tumbling.

Their slow and constantly impeded progress took its toll on both the renegades, and even took a lesser toll on Jessie. Snatcher grew short of breath and was forced to call for frequent halts. Even Caleb showed signs that he'd begun to feel the strain of carrying both rifles in addition to pushing ahead and breaking trail. Jessie herself was tired and felt a bit bruised from having bounced now and then when Snatcher made one of his frequent missteps.

They'd covered perhaps three quarters of a mile. The sun was high enough now to send its rays down in a slant when the undergrowth ended as abruptly as though it had been slashed away with axes and grub hoes. Beyond a boggy stretch, where amidst a ground-hugging cover of broad-leafed vines several small green-mossed puddles of water glinted in the sunlight, a ramshackle hut stood. Close behind it was the ragged line of higher-growth brush that enclosed the little clearing.

When Caleb started around the perimeter of the boggy area and Snatcher followed, Jessie was certain that they'd finally reached their destination. They were within a half dozen paces from the hut when a bearded man stepped out of its open doorway. His slouch hat was pulled down low, and with the sun at his back Jessie could make out few details of his face. He hefted a rifle in one hand. A pair of ammunition-filled bandoliers were draped on his shoulders and crossed on his chest, and a holstered revolver dangled low on his right thigh.

"Where the devil have you men been?" he asked. His voice had all the smoothness of a nutmeg grater. "And what in hell are you doing bringing a woman in here? You know that's against orders!"

"We didn't have much else to do with her except shoot her where we found her," Caleb replied. "But me and Snatcher was going to bring her to you soon as we could, Mr. Flynn."

"After you'd finished with her, maybe," Flynn said. His voice was edged with sarcasm that did not match his wide grin, which revealed a double row of yellow snaggling teeth. "Well, put her in your shack out of the way while we do our talking."

Snatcher and Caleb exchanged glances, then Snatcher moved on to the hut. He turned sideways and ducked to carry Jessie through the doorway. In the shadowed light of the little shack's interior she saw a pair of chairs, a small stove, a table and a low double bed. Snatcher dumped her on the bed and went back outside.

Jessie could hear Flynn's voice very clearly as he said, "All right. Go on and spin me your yarn. After I've heard it, I'll decide how much of it I can believe and how bad you're lying."

"Well, it's like this," Caleb replied. "I was keeping

watch by the creek yesterday evening, just like you told us we was to do. Snatcher was sleeping here in the shack till it got to be time for him to come spell me. Then I seen this boat coming up the creek—"

"What boat?" Flynn broke in.

"Just an old dugout, Mr. Flynn. It wasn't no different to any dugout I ever seen here in the Thicket. Anyhow, there was that big Tonkawa in it, and there was another fellow; he wasn't nowhere big as the Tonk. I never seen him before, so I don't reckon he belongs here. Then there was this woman that we got over there in the shack right now."

Caleb stopped for breath after his lengthy speech of explanation, and Snatcher picked up the thread of their story.

"That woman don't belong in the Thicket, neither," he said. "If she did, I'd've run into her before now."

"Yes, I know your reputation, Snatcher," Flynn said drily. "Now let Caleb go on with what he was telling me."

"There ain't much left to tell," Caleb continued. "When I seen them three, I figured right off that the Tonkawa had gone and got them other two from someplace, to help him. So I begun shooting, like I was supposed to—"

"I hope you got rid of the men," Flynn broke in.

"Well . . ." Caleb hesitated, then went on, "I wasn't that lucky. The light wasn't real good for shooting that time of day; it was shading down to dark by then."

"You didn't even get one of them?" Flynn frowned.

Caleb shook his head. "Like I said, it wasn't light enough to see good. Anyways, the big redskin moved the boat real fast and they went back down the creek."

"And you didn't have sense enough to follow them and keep shooting till you got rid of them?" Flynn demanded when Caleb paused for breath.

"Well, I didn't follow 'em long. It popped into my head that if they wasn't dead set on coming in the Thicket they'd go back to where they come from. But then I figured that since the big redskin was along, they might go upstream to the next branch and bring their canoe up it. So I come back here to git Snatcher and both of us cut through the Thicket to the other creek."

Inside the cabin, a number of things were beginning to come together in Jessie's mind. It was obvious from the conversation she'd overheard so far that both Caleb and Snatcher had been hired by the timber pirates. Reminding herself that she'd have time to consider later the ideas that were occurring to her now, she concentrated on listening to the conversation that was continuing outside the shanty.

"So me and Snatcher got there too late to git at 'em while they was easy targets out in the boat," Caleb was continuing. "We figured we'd be there first and could potshot 'em while they was still in the boat, but they'd beat us there and was already ashore. When me and Snatcher begun trying to pick 'em off, they turned out to be better shots than we'd calculated, so we pulled back to where we could bushwhack 'em while they was crossing the big burn. We followed 'em there, but they run into that swamp-rat named Barkey. Now, me and Snatcher was close enough to hear what they said, but we wasn't where we could pick 'em off easy. When we heard 'em talking about the men going back to the boat to get their gear and leaving the woman in that cave, we figured the smartest thing we could do was grab off the woman."

"And you didn't bring her to me, so you must've decided you'd play your cards close to your chest," Flynn said. His voice was bland and noncommittal.

"I guess I don't follow you," Caleb replied. His voice had a strain of worry in it that he'd been able to disguise before.

"You figured to hold on to her and have a few days of

fun," Flynn went on. "Isn't that about the way it stacks up?"

"Well, what if we did?" Snatcher broke in defiantly. "We caught the bitch, dammit! We got some fun coming to us!"

"When you're on my pay sheet you have fun when I say you can!" Flynn snapped. "Do you understand that, or will I have to get some of my boys to beat it into your heads that as long as you're drawing down a pay packet from me, I'm your boss and you're going to do what I say?"

"Oh, we know that, Mr. Flynn!" Snatcher replied quickly. "We wasn't gonna keep the woman here long."

"I've got my doubts about how long you'd've kept her if I hadn't just happened to be here when you showed up with her," Flynn replied. "But I'll overlook that and get on with what I came here for. Mr. Stone's just come back from Houston, and he wants everybody on this job to be at the main camp tomorrow right after sunset. He's got a few things to tell you."

"Things like what?" Caleb frowned.

"You'll learn that tomorrow night," Flynn answered. "But I'll tell you this much now. He's brought a barrel of first-rate whiskey back with him, and from what he told me, he's going to pass it out real free."

"Like he done the first time he talked to us?" Snatcher asked. "I swear to you, that was about the finest whiskey I ever poured down my guzzle!"

"Snatcher's right," Caleb agreed. "It was real prime stuff. I wouldn't mind tasting some more of it again myself."

"Well, you'll get all of it you can hold, tomorrow night," Flynn promised. "Now, I'm of two minds about that woman in your shanty over there." He paused, frowning.

"Meaning what?" Snatcher asked after a moment had passed and Flynn still had not said anything more.

"Meaning first of all that you're right about her not belonging here in the Thicket," Flynn went on. "And since she's come here with the Tonkawa, she might just be from the Indian Agency or some outfit like that."

"I guess I don't follow you," Caleb prompted when Flynn did not go on.

"If she's from the Indian Agency, they'll start wondering about her if she doesn't get back when she's supposed to," Flynn explained. "They're not about to let anybody who works for them just drop out of sight. They'll have a U.S. marshal or one of their own men from the Indian Police come looking for her."

"Well, now. If she's down in the bottom of the river or one of the big creeks, the alligators won't leave much of her to find," Snatcher suggested.

"I've already thought about that." Flynn nodded. "But we don't want that to happen."

"It wouldn't be the first time something like that happened here," Caleb said. His words came out slowly and there was reluctance showing in the tone of his voice.

"Maybe not," Flynn agreed. "But right now's no time to draw attention to the Thicket. If you get the Federals in here looking for her, there's not much way of telling what else they'll stumble across."

"Meaning the job you got us here to do?" Caleb suggested.

"That and a lot more," Flynn replied. "And there's also those three men. They'll be casting around looking for her if they get back to where they left her and she's not there."

"Well, you're the boss," Caleb said. He put no inflection of any sort on his words. They came out flat and emotionless.

"Yes," Flynn agreed. "But don't you men forget for a minute that I'm in the same fix as you are. I've got a boss looking over what I do, just like I ride herd on you."

"You tell us what to do," Caleb suggested. "One way or the other, me and Snatcher'll see it gets done."

"It's too late to take her back and just dump her where you found her," Flynn said thoughtfully. "Chances are she's heard every word we've said out here; she'll know too much by now for us to risk turning her loose. I guess you men better have your fun with her tonight. And I don't want you to tell me anything or hear you say anything about her when you come to the main camp tomorrow. Do you understand me?"

"I reckon," Caleb said. "How about you, Snatcher?"

"It don't look like I got much to say about it," Snatcher replied. "All of us is up the same damn tree."

"All right," Flynn told them. "I've got to go on now and get the word about tomorrow night to the other fellows that're spread around. You do whatever you've got to, and be sure that you don't get drunk enough to blab a lot tomorrow night."

Jessie, lying helpless on the evil-smelling bed inside the cabin and listening to the three men talking outside, felt an icy shiver travel along her spine as she heard Flynn's words. She tested her bonds again, knowing in advance that her efforts were wasted. Then she heard the scraping of her captors' footsteps as they moved toward the door of the shanty.

Chapter 9

"Jessie's not in the cave, Fletache!" Ki said, frowning as he came back into the sunlight. "And if she'd started to backtrack and meet us, we'd surely have run into her. The trail we left coming here was plain enough."

"Then she must have left for some reason we don't know yet," the Tonkawa said. He turned and scanned the burned-over area for a moment, then said to Ki and Barkey, "She couldn't have cut across the burn, or there'd be torn vines between the stumps to mark her trail."

"Where did she go, then?" Ki asked. "Knowing that we'd be coming back, she wouldn't have left here without some very good reason."

"First we must find her trail," Fletache replied. He turned to Barkey. "You're almost as good a tracker as I am, Jeff. Let us start from the cave and circle around the burn in different directions and find her tracks."

"I'll go back and take a closer look inside the cave," Ki volunteered. "She might've left some sign or message for us in there. I was so surprised when I didn't find her asleep that I didn't take time to look around."

Ki went back into the cavern. He waited for his eyes to adjust to the twilight dimness of the big arched chamber, then started examining its firm dirt floor. Had Ki not been a very skillful tracker indeed, he might have missed the small disturbed area near the middle of the cavern where Jessie had lain down to sleep. The first sign he noticed was the narrow oval impression made in the dirt floor by her rifle butt when she'd leaned on it while she lay down. Then he saw the long tapered mark where Jessie had placed the rifle, and along one side of the long thin groove it had left there were prints of her boot heels below a pressed-down patch where she'd lain.

From that starting point, the rest was comparatively easy. Moving on his hands and knees, Ki crawled in a wide arc around the place where he was sure Jessie had laid down to nap. He held his head slantwise, close to the floor, always keeping his eyes toward the oval-shaped pool of light that filtered in from the cave's mouth.

As he moved now, he could see other footprints in addition to those Jessie had left. They were the prints left by the boots of Caleb and Snatcher, with Jessie's smaller and less well defined footprints between them, marking their progress to the mouth of the cave.

"Jessie was taken away by two men," Ki told Fletache when the Tonkawa returned.

Fletache nodded. "Yes. Jeff is now looking for the trail they left when they took her away."

"Then don't let's waste any time catching up with him," Ki said quickly. "We must hurry and join him."

"He won't have gone very far. Did you find anything else in the cave?"

Ki shook his head. "Jessie didn't leave any clues for us, if that's what you mean. The tracks show that she lay down to sleep, and the two men captured her before she could move or try to get away. She must have been very tired, or they wouldn't have been able to surprise her the way the footprints in the cave show they did. And I'm sure they must have been holding a gun on her, or she'd have put up a fight."

Fletache had started moving while Ki was still talking, and by the time Ki had finished they were circling the rim of the rock outcrop behind the cave opening. They reached the narrow strip of softer ground that lay between the burned-over area and a tangle of tall brush ahead. The Tonkawa pointed to an area of soft soil where footprints showed in a confused overlapping tangle. Ki was just beginning to unravel the pattern of the prints when Fletache spoke again.

"Here you can see what they did," he told Ki. "One of the men picked Jessie up to carry her on his shoulders, and the other went ahead."

As Ki bent to look at the footprints, Fletache whistled, a strange lilting noise that sounded like a bird's call. In a moment an answering whistle sounded from the bushes ahead of him.

"Good." The Tonkawa nodded. "Jeff has found something. It must be the trail left by the men who have Jessie. Let me lead the way from here, Ki. I can take us in a straight line to where Jeff is."

Without waiting for Ki's reply, Fletache began pushing his way through the thick growth. Ki followed, his hands busy trying to catch the long, face-stinging twigs of the wiry long-stemmed bushes that Fletache pushed aside as he advanced.

Soon they could hear the rustlings ahead of them that told of Jeff Barkey's progress, and within a few more minutes they saw him—or at least the suggestion of his outline—through the tangled maze of vegetation ahead.

They'd made no effort to move silently or to hide their presence, and it was obvious that Jeff had heard them in their branch-snapping progress and had stopped to wait for them to join him.

"I got a pretty good idee where they're heading for," he told Ki and Fletache as they reached him. "And that's give me a hunch who taken Miss Starbuck. It's likely to've been Caleb and that Snatcher fellow. They got a cabin a ways ahead"—he was pointing as he spoke—"right off in that direction."

"Of course." Fletache nodded. "I know them and where their cabin is." He turned to Ki. "It is not far, but we would be wise to circle when we get close to it and come on these men from behind. They are both killers. I would not like to risk Jessie's life by giving them time to—"

"I understand what you're saying, Fletache," Ki broke in. "And the Thicket's your home territory. Go the way you think is best, whichever it is, to move in on them and surprise them."

Fletache turned to Jeff Barkey, who nodded without speaking and turned to continue in the direction he'd been moving. Ki and the big Tonkawa fell in behind him. They started forward at a fast walk, pushing through trackless undergrowth, heedless of the thin, wiry branches that whipped their raised arms and occasionally landed with sharp stings on their faces.

It was apparent to Ki that Barkey knew his way around in the Big Thicket as well as Fletache did. Although Ki could see faint traces now and then of the trail along which Barkey was leading them, there were stretches where the chest-high green grasses and the wide-spreading growth of tall snagging brush and the trailing tendrils of vines hid the ground completely. Ki got the feeling he was wading—or more properly, swimming—through muddy green water instead of walking on dry land.

Several times they passed through small groves of trees, few of which Ki could identify. He was familiar with pine trees from his travels in the West with Jessie and her father, and could distinguish them by their needles and cones, though not all the pine trees he saw were cone-bearers.

Though the pines were tall and thin, and offered no barriers to their passage, there were other trees that more closely resembled huge spreading bushes. These sprawled with their limbs shooting out only chest-high, or head-high, and in such stands their progress slowed. Ki and Fletache were forced to push aside the branches, which whipped back after Jeff had shouldered through them, and dodge or catch the whipping branches before the supple growth could snap like lashes and cut into their unprotected faces.

In a few places some of the trees and most of the bushes rose only a few feet above Ki's head, and these could be passed through with relative ease. Elsewhere, they walked through broad stands of towering trees from which the vines hung like curtains to meet the lower ground cover. Many of the trees had boles bigger around than his chest. The most troublesome patches of ground were the treeless areas where vines covered the ground calf-high and grabbed at their ankles as they crossed on ground that in most such stretches was soft and soggy and treacherous underfoot.

They had just crossed one of the soggy stretches and another stand of trees thrusting up from a ground cover of thin-leafed ferns loomed ahead. Ki saw Jeff stop and raise his arm, then wave ahead with his open palm, a gesture that he took to mean that Jeff wanted him and Fletache to catch up. Fletache stopped when he reached Jeff's side and Ki joined them a moment later.

"That cabin Caleb and Snatcher lives in is just a little ways ahead," Jeff told them.

Fletache nodded. "This is close to the place where I remembered it to be. I am sure now that it's the same one. And there are no others close by."

"What do you figure is the best way to work this out?" Jeff went on.

"Let's move closer and look," Ki suggested. "You've both seen the place, but I haven't. I'd like to get some idea of what we'll be getting into."

Moving as a group now, the trio advanced carefully through the thinning brush. They saw the cabin after they'd moved only a dozen careful steps. Ki frowned when he got his first look at the stretch of boggy, water-dotted soil that lay between them and their objective. He scanned the sides of the swampy area.

Along one edge of a muddy sump hole there was a narrow strip of solid land, but on the other the dense tangle of green ran all the way into the water. The path that was dimly visible around the clear side was a bit wider in front of the cabin than elsewhere, but beyond the little ramshackle structure the brush grew thick between the trunks of a grove of tall taper-trunked cypress trees that were apparently rooted close behind it.

"There is no easy way to get to the cabin," Fletache said. "The water keeps us from going directly to it. I know how deep the mud below the surface must be. We do not dare risk using the path, there. If I was one of those two in the cabin, I would be watching it very carefully."

"We could yell at 'em from here and cut 'em down when they come out the door," Jeff suggested.

"No!" Ki replied quickly. "If we have to use our guns,

we must be very careful about shooting. Jessie is almost certainly inside, and we cannot risk harming her. If we begin shooting, those men will shoot back, and we have no good place to take cover."

"I sorta forgot we'd want to look out for Miss Jessie if push come to shove," Jeff said.

Fletache was frowning thoughtfully. He said, "At the back of the cabin the brush grows close. One of us should circle to approach the hut from that direction."

"Jeff, do you think you can circle around to the right-hand side and push through that brush to the cabin?" Ki asked.

"Sure. It'll be bound to take me a little while, but I can do that easy as falling offen a log."

"Perhaps I should go with Jeff," Fletache suggested. "He can stop at the side and help you when you reach the door, and I will find my way around the end of the cabin to its back."

"Good enough," Ki agreed. "And while you're doing that, I'll move *ninja*-style to the front along the path. I can promise that no one in the cabin will see me."

"Then give Jeff and me time to get in place before you go any closer to the building," Fletache said. "Do you know the call of the fish crow, Ki?"

"I know what a crow sounds like," Ki replied. "Is a fish crow any different from other kinds?"

"Very little," Fletache told him. "It is a higher-pitched cawing, but it is still a caw."

Before Ki could reply, the big Tonkawa stretched his lips and flattened them and let out the *caw-caw-caw* of a crow.

Ki nodded. "I'll know it when I hear it again. You and Jeff go ahead, then, Fletache. I'll listen for your caw, then

I'll take to the path. I'll only need a few minutes to get to the cabin."

Inside the cabin, Jessie looked covertly at the two men who sat at the battered table, a bottle of whiskey on the tabletop. They did not seem to miss the niceties of such things as glasses. First Caleb, then Snatcher, tilted the bottle without even bothering to wipe off its neck as it passed from one to the other. After the conversation she'd overheard, first between Flynn and the pair and now between the two of them, she had no illusions about the fate they were considering for her.

She was far from being resigned to what seemed to loom ahead in the immediate future, and had no intention of giving up or submitting tamely. She'd been cudgeling her brain for a way to free herself, but all her thinking had been short-lived when she came up against the reality of her situation. She turned her mind away from the thoughts that had been churning through it to concentrate on what the pair at the table were discussing.

"Damn that nosey Flynn!" Snatcher was saying. "Ain't it just my damn bad luck he'd be waiting here when we brought in this dame! Why couldn't he've come yesterday?"

"It's not going to do you a bit of good to bellyache," Caleb replied. "If you want the money this job we got is going to bring in, you'll have to do what he said."

"I don't argue agin you, Caleb. Both of us has seen him tear into some poor devil that didn't do what he was supposed to, and I don't aim to git my nose bashed flat and my ribs busted up. But that don't mean I like losing all the fun we could've had for the next two or three months, not taking to count the extra cash we stood to make."

"Kiss all of that goodbye like a man, Snatcher," Caleb

advised. "Cash money's no good anyhow, except if you've got a saloon or fancy-house to spend it in."

"I guess. Well, since the woman ain't going to be around the way we figured, who gets first crack at her? You or me?"

"I don't guess it makes a lot of difference, does it?"

"No, but like my mammy used to say to Grandmam, age before beauty. All you got to do is say so if you wanta go first."

"Seems to me the fair way'd be to cut cards," Caleb suggested. "If that suits you—"

"It's better'n argufying over who'll be first," Snatcher agreed. "I'll fetch the deck."

Jessie watched while the younger man got up and rummaged along the shelves that were nailed to the wall behind the stove. He came back to the table carrying a dog-eared deck of playing cards and dropped it in front of Caleb.

"You wanta shuffle?" he asked. "Or just cut the way the deck stands now?"

"My old pappy was a right smart man when it come to playing cards," Caleb replied. "He learned me to shuffle and cut any time I was in a gamble."

"Go ahead and shuffle, then."

Caleb picked up the cards and shuffled them, then cut the deck. He shoved it across to Snatcher as he said, "Seeing as I shuffled, it's jest fair you get first pick."

Snatcher slid a card from the middle of the deck. He turned it faceup on the table, and when the face of the queen of hearts was revealed a satisfied chuckle came from his throat. "You'll have to go pretty good to beat that one, Caleb," he said. "It'll take a king or an ace."

From the bed where she lay bound, Jessie could not see the tabletop. Nevertheless, she watched with growing anger as Caleb selected his card. He laid it beside the one Snatcher had drawn.

"Well, now," he said. "Looks like you'll be the one to take a long walk outside, Snatcher. I got you beat."

"Dammit!" Snatcher grumbled. "Eight cards in that fool deck that'd top mine, and you had to be lucky enough to pull one of 'em! All right, Caleb. I ain't going to fuss, fair's fair. I'll go out and prowl around. Long as that's what I got to do, I might as well take along my rifle and see if I can pick off a couple of squirrels we can have for supper."

Kicking away the chair he'd been using, Snatcher picked up his rifle and started for the door.

Ki and Jeff Barkey stood at the edge of the clearing, hidden from the cabin door by the dense, head-high stand of honey locust and possumhaw bushes, waiting for Fletache to circle around the cabin to its rear.

It seemed to both of them that the big Tonkawa was taking a lot of time. Even after he'd gotten clear of the grabbing branches of the shrubbery and reached the edge of the marshy ground where he could move almost silently at the edge of the big cypress trees that rose from the water-soaked ground, they could still hear the occasional squishy sigh of his feet pulling free from the clinging mud.

At last the faint noises of Fletache's movements died away, and the calls of birds and occasional high-pitched complaining chatter of the squirrels that his passage had disturbed also faded into silence. Now and then a shrill chatter sounded from one of the frolicking squirrels, but now the frisky little animals were only chasing one another through the branches of the tall cypress trees. No other sounds broke the silence.

"Fletache ought to be in place at the back of the cabin

by now," Ki said. Even though he spoke in a half whisper his voice sounded loud.

"If he is, we better stir our stumps and get moving, too," Jeff suggested.

Ki noddcd. Then, though he urgently wanted to reach their objective, he stepped aside to let Jeff take the lead as they started along the border of the wet, yielding ground. They reached the place where the soggy soil gave way to firmer footing, and Ki reached forward to grasp Jeff's shoulder.

"I'll go in front of you now," he said. "You stop at that big bush ahead and take cover."

"You figure to go up against them two without a gun?" Jeff frowned.

"Of course. I have other weapons. But my *shuriken* must be used at close range, and I can move silently, without being seen."

Though it was obvious from the expression on Jeff Barkey's face that he harbored a large stock of disbelief, he stepped aside without protest and let Ki take the lead.

To one as skilled in *ninjitsu* as Ki, covering the sixty or seventy yards that remained between him and the cabin was child's play. He flitted from the concealment of one bush to the next, his dark clothing merging with the deep shadows cast by the nooning sun. He'd covered more than half the distance to the cabin door when Snatcher came out. Ki saw the rifle in the other man's hand, and almost at the same time he saw Fletache flit from the dense growth directly behind the cabin.

A moment later a loud raucous birdcall came from the area where Fletache had disappeared. Though he had no way to return the signal, Ki was certain that once he'd started an attack, the big Tonkawa would move instantly.

Slipping a *shuriken* from his vest pocket, he launched the wicked blade in its deadly whirling path.

Ki's aiming point was Snatcher's throat, vulnerable and bared because his shirt collar was not buttoned, and the star-pointed steel blade spun in a silent shining arc toward its target. Whether his outlaw training had honed Snatcher's sense of danger, or whether he saw the glinting blade spinning toward him, Snatcher brought up his rifle and fired. The *shuriken* struck the gun's forestock and grated on the barrel while the outlaw was triggering off his shot.

Behind him, Ki heard the report of Jeff's rifle. The slug took Snatcher in the chest. Its impact threw him back against a sapling that was growing a yard or so from the cabin wall. He stood leaning against the little tree for a split second, then began a slow, sliding fall that ended when he slumped into a motionless heap on the ground.

Chapter 10

Ki had already taken two or three steps toward the cabin when he heard Jeff groan and turned to look back. He saw Jeff lying on the ground, trying to sit up. Knowing that Fletache was already at the cabin to help Jessie, Ki went back to his companion. Jeff was trying to lift himself off the ground, but his left arm dangled limply and he was unable to turn easily enough to lever himself up with his right.

"How bad did he get you?" Ki asked.

"I been hurt worse," Jeff responded. "But I guess I'm gonna need a little bit of help."

Ki bent over and extended his hand. Jeff grasped it and brought himself to his feet. Immediately Ki turned his attention to the young man's wounded arm. The bullet had gone into the fleshy upper curve of Jeff's left arm and creased it deeply. A long, bloody line marked its path, where the slug had touched the bone of his shoulder blade and been deflected through the thin layer of flesh that covered it.

"You're going to have a sore arm and shoulder for a

while, until this hole heals," Ki said. "But it's not going to hamper you. In fact, it could've been a whole lot worse."

He'd taken his *tanto* from its sheath while he was talking. With the knife's thin, razor-sharp blade he made a quick small nick to remove the lead bullet. Then he slit around the armhole seam of Jeff's shirtsleeve with the *tanto*'s tip. Sliding the sleeve from the young man's wounded arm, he fashioned a makeshift bandage around the arm and shoulder which covered the angry red line of the bullet crease.

"This will keep you from bleeding," Ki went on as he knotted the cloth around the wound. "But you won't be doing much rifle shooting for a spell."

"I ain't figuring to. I—I guess I feel a little bit funny right now, Ki," Jeff replied. He was silent for a moment, then went on, "I've done my share of hunting deer, and there's been two times when I've shot me a bear. But I never did shoot at a man and kill him before now."

"All you can do is put it out of your mind. You had every right to shoot him, though," Ki assured him. "He didn't waste any time shooting you."

"I guess. Anyways, I wasn't the one that shot first, and that makes me feel some better."

"Just don't think about it," Ki advised. "Now, let's get on to the cabin and see what's happened to Jessie and Fletache."

Inside the cabin, Jessie had listened to the conversation between Caleb and Snatcher as they discussed her fate. Though she was certain that by now Ki and Fletache would have discovered she'd been captured, and equally certain they were on their way to free her, thoughts of what the pair sitting at the table were planning for her, and the memory of their conversation with Flynn, increased her urgency to escape.

She tested her bonds for the twentieth time, knowing before she did so that they would be no more yielding now than they'd been in the beginning of her captivity. Then she tried chewing at the bandana that Snatcher had used to gag her, but it was as tightly knotted as the ropes on her arms and ankles. At last Jessie abandoned her efforts. She watched and listened while Caleb and Snatcher gambled for her. As soon as Snatcher had picked up his rifle and reached the door of the cabin, Caleb came to the bed.

"You ain't got no reason to be fearful," he said. His voice was pitched low, for Snatcher was just going through the door. Jerking his head toward his partner's disappearing back, Caleb went on, "Wait till he gets away far enough so's he can't hear us talking. Then we'll figure something out."

Before Jessie could reply, two closely spaced shots broke the silence outside. Caleb spanned the distance to the door in three long strides. He peered out cautiously, then came back to the bed. This time he untied the bandana around Jessie's jaws.

When he'd finally finished working the knotted kerchief free, Jessie's first words were, "What happened outside? Who was Snatcher shooting at? Or was it somebody else shooting at him?"

Before replying, Caleb took his big bowie knife from its sheath and began sawing at the rope that held her arms.

"It was both," he told her. "It looks like to me that them friends of yours tracked after me and Snatcher. There's a Chinee fellow, and I reckon the big Indian's with him. Anyhow, it looks like Snatcher tried to stop 'em and they got the best of him. They'll be here to get you in just a few minutes."

"And your friend Snatcher?" she asked.

"He's stretched out in front of the cabin. Looks to me like he ain't gonna get up, neither."

"Dead?"

Caleb nodded. "I figure."

"Your friend getting killed doesn't seem to bother you."

"We wasn't rightly what you'd call friends. We just sorta hung around together because there wasn't nobody else for either one of us to hang around with."

"What about you?" she asked. "Are you just letting me go because you're afraid Ki and Fletache will kill you?"

"I don't figure they're that sort," Caleb replied. "Which don't mean I aim to take no fool chances."

He finally severed the rope that had secured Jessie's wrists. She began flexing her fingers to get the feeling back into them. Caleb moved to the foot of the bed and started cutting the rope around her ankles.

"You heard everything me and Snatcher said, and you got to believe me," Caleb told Jessie as he worked. "Him and me's just been partnering a little while, but I've already found out I don't cotton to him the way I figured I would when we teamed up. You seen how all of this was his scheme. I just went along with him so's not to put no trouble in between us."

"I noticed you weren't very enthusiastic about his ideas," Jessie agreed. "I was beginning to hope you might figure out a way to let me go."

"There wasn't much I could do, long as Snatcher was around to hear everything you and me might say. And if I was figuring out things the way he did, I'd be standing right now in that door over there. I'd have my rifle and be shooting at your friends."

"What're you going to do, then?"

"I've done all I can, now I've cut you free. The rest of it's up to you."

"I'm afraid I don't understand you."

"I got a pretty good hunch them friends of yours are going to come in shooting," Caleb said. He reached for the heavy cast-iron skillet that stood on the stove. Holding it out to Jessie, he went on, "Here. Hit me on the head with it."

"I don't—" Jessie began.

Caleb broke in, "If I don't look like I'm dead when they come in, I figure I'm likely to be dead for sure. Now hit me, ma'am, please. They won't bother me if I'm laid out, and you'll have time to tell 'em what really went on."

Through Jessie's mind there flashed a sudden vivid picture of Ki coming in with a *shuriken* in his hand or Fletache bursting through the doorway with his rifle. Suddenly what Caleb asked her to do made sense. She took the skillet and landed a side-swiping blow on his head.

Although Jessie tried not to hit too hard, the weight of the heavy cast-iron pan put more impact than she'd intended into her stroke. Caleb dropped like a poleaxed ox. He was stretched out unconscious when Ki burst in with Jeff at his heels. Before either of them could speak, Fletache came running through the doorway.

Ki had a *shuriken* in his hand ready to launch, and Fletache's forefinger was curled around the trigger of his rifle. Both of them stopped instantly when they saw Jessie standing beside Caleb's prone form, the big skillet in her hand.

"How on earth did you manage to get free and knock him out, Jessie?" Ki asked.

"I didn't. Caleb cut the ropes I was tied up with and gave me this skillet to hit him with."

"You mean—" Ki began.

Jessie cut him short. "I mean exactly what I said," she replied. "Caleb asked me to hit him and knock him out."

During the dangerous and adventurous years when Jessie and Ki had worked in close partnership battling the hired thugs of the cartel, they'd encountered even more unlikely situations. Ki merely nodded and accepted Jessie's explanation. Fletache's face was still drawn into the puzzled frown which had appeared on it as Jessie explained.

"But why would he do that?" he asked.

"He was afraid you and Ki and Jeff would come in shooting. I suppose that's what his partner would've done," Jessie said.

"His partner's fired his last shot," Ki told her. "But he managed to wound Jeff with it."

"It ain't too bad, Miss Jessie," Jeff protested as Jessie turned to him. "My arm don't hurt hardly at all."

"Then I'll wait to fix it properly until Ki and Fletache and I get a few things straightened out," Jessie said. "And I'd say what we need to do first is get Caleb back on his feet and find out everything he knows about the timber pirates. From what I overheard, I'm almost certain that they're getting ready to clear-cut the Thicket."

Caleb was beginning to stir when Jessie bent over him. She looked around at the kitchen area of the little cabin and saw a bucket of water and a grimy towel on a bench a short distance from the stove. She stepped over to it and sloshed the towel in the bucket until it was dripping, then swabbed Caleb's face. He stirred after she'd passed it over his face a few times. Then his eyes opened and he looked up at her.

"For a pretty young lady, you sure got a lot of muscle," he said wryly. "I didn't figure you'd land such a good one on me."

"I'm sorry I hit you so hard," she said. "That skillet was a lot heavier than I realized."

"Oh, I ain't complaining," Caleb told her quickly. He sat up and fingered the big bump that had formed where the skillet landed. His fingers hit an exceptionally sore spot and he winced. He got to his feet as he went on, "Anyways, when I seen Snatcher laying out there dead, I figured a knot on the head was a sight better'n a bullet in my gizzard."

"I suppose it is, when you think about it that way." Ki nodded.

"I'd better do something about that knot," Jessie broke in. "Ki, suppose you and Fletache build a fire in the stove and heat some clean water. I imagine there's a spring close to the cabin. I'll make up a hot poultice to put on Caleb's head, and I'll tend to Jeff's arm at the same time. I imagine that bullet wound is beginning to bother him."

"It ain't really such a much, ma'am," Jeff assured her. "Oh, it's starting to sting a little bit, not enough to bother me a lot. But if we're going to be dodging around trying to do something about them timber pirates, I'll sure need to be in shape to handle a gun."

"From what I overheard when their boss was here talking to Caleb and Snatcher, they aren't going to do anything until after they have some sort of meeting tomorrow night." Jessie frowned. "So we'll have a little bit of time."

"This is something new," Ki said. "What kind of meeting, Jessie? And where?"

"Things have been happening so fast there hasn't been time to tell you everything, Ki," Jessie replied. "And I'm sure that Caleb knows more about the meeting than I do; it seems they had something of the kind before."

"That was when them tree pirates was trying to buy up all the squatters' rights us folks in the Thicket has," Caleb put in. "There was a lot of talk about the boards cut from some of the trees being worth more'n the land, and how much money we'd stand to get if we sold out to 'em. But nobody ever showed us no real money, not even a dime."

"When was this meeting?" Jessie asked.

Caleb frowned thoughtfully. "Seems to me it was about the time the spider lilies bloomed. I guess you've found out by now that us Thicket folks don't pay much mind to calendars and clocks. But it'd be close to a year back." Turning to Fletache he asked, "Ain't that right?"

Fletache nodded and said to Jessie, "A year ago is close enough. But the tree cutters did not come here to go to work until much later. Even then, there were only a few who went all over the Thicket looking at the trees. It was after that they had the meeting."

"Timber cruisers"—Jessie nodded—"sent out to locate the areas where the best trees are growing. Did they offer to buy the land that the people here were living on?"

Fletache shook his head. "No. And they did not promise that the land our homes were on would not be taken from us, either. That is when I began to think of asking Alex Starbuck for help."

"It seems to me that we'd better have a meeting of our own, while we're all here," Jessie decided. "The timber pirates won't be doing anything before tomorrow night, so we don't have to hurry. Let's get Snatcher buried and fix up Jeff and Caleb before we start talking. Ki, suppose you and Fletache build a fire and find some clean water. After I've gotten them bandaged up, we'll put our heads together and start talking about what we should do. Then we'll see what sort of plan we can come up with."

A busy hour later, the little group sat down in the cabin. During that hour, Ki and Fletache had put Snatcher's body to rest in a grave dug in the soft earth behind the cabin. Jessie had spent her time binding a poultice of scraped swamp-willow bark to Jeff's arm and shoulder, and had given Caleb her spare bandana to soak in cold water and hold to the bulging knot on his head.

"It's too late for us to do much of anything else today," she said. "What we've got to think about now is that meeting Caleb and Snatcher are supposed to attend tomorrow night."

"Flynn acted like he'd be real mad if we wasn't there," Caleb volunteered. "But he didn't say much about what him and his bunch figured to do at it, besides put away a lot of whiskey and wake up with a headache the next morning."

"You mentioned that this Flynn said the meeting was going to be like the first one," Jessie went on. "From what Fletache told Ki and me, the lumbermen spent most of their time trying to persuade you and your friends in the Thicket to move."

Caleb nodded. "That was before they put up that monstrous big building."

"A building?" Fletache frowned. "They had no building when I left to go find Alex Starbuck and ask him for help."

"Well, they sure put one up while you was gone," Caleb said. "They clear-cut a big stand of virgin pine to get the logs to build it with. I didn't feel a bit right about them fellows when I seen all the stumps, and I didn't like to hear how they was talking, neither. They said there wasn't going to be much left of the Thicket when they got finished cutting. Said they'd pay us enough to git off so's we could buy places to settle somewhere else. There wasn't many of us that believed 'em."

"I did not believe them," Fletache volunteered. "And if they have started to cut trees, they mean to stay."

"They sure ain't got no kind feelings left towards us," Caleb put in. "That's why me and Snatcher sorta had a falling-out about it when we got to talking after Flynn left. Snatcher was still mad when Ki and Jeff showed up. I reckon that's why he begun shooting."

"How about you, Caleb?" Jessie asked. "You and Snatcher seemed to be working together pretty well when you caught me in the cave and brought me here."

"I been doing a lot of thinking since then, Miss Jessie," Caleb answered. "Especially after what Flynn said. Why, the only place I got to call home is here in the Thicket. I just don't know how I'd git along somewheres else."

"And I already know how you feel, Fletache," Jessie went on, turning to the big Tonkawa. She looked at Jeff. "I suppose you feel the same way?"

He nodded. "I sure do, ma'am. Folks like me generally does, folks born here like I was. I sure don't want to move, and I don't wanta see all the trees in the Thicket chopped down, neither."

For a moment Jessie sat in thoughtful, frowning silence. Then she looked at Ki and said, "You and I would never be able to fool anybody into accepting us as Thicket dwellers. We can't go to that meeting the timbermen are having tomorrow night. Even if there's a big crowd, we'd still stand out like a pair of sore thumbs."

Ki nodded. "You're certainly right about that, Jessie. I suppose you have something in mind for us to do, though?"

"Of course. I'm not sure how it'll all work out. Caleb's changed his mind about working for the timbermen, but there's no reason for him to tell them about it yet."

"I ain't a bit ashamed of how I feel, Jessie!" Caleb broke in to protest. "I'm ready to stand up and be counted!"

"This isn't quite the right time for you to let them find out that you're not going to work for them again," Jessie said quickly. She turned to Jeff and went on, "All of us know that you feel the way Caleb does, Jeff. But the more we can learn about their plans, the easier it's going to be for us to spoil them. What would you think about Caleb taking you with him to that meeting the timbermen are having tomorrow night?"

"You mean you want us to be—well, sorta, spies?" Caleb broke in.

"I suppose you could call it that." She nodded. "Fletache certainly can't let them catch sight of him."

"No," the big Tonkawa agreed. "Even if many men attend, I would be seen at once, and the lumber people have no liking for me. But I will stay in the brush close by, and be ready to help if there is trouble."

"I think that's what Ki and I must do, too," Jessie said. "We can find a way to hide. But since we don't know anything except that they'll be having a meeting, Ki and I might not be able to get close enough to hear what's said, either."

"Well, now," Caleb said, his face knotted into a thoughtful frown, "I ain't so sure I'd be much good at snooping."

"We could swing it between the two of us, Caleb," Jeff told the older man. "I can see what Miss Jessie's aiming for."

"I reckon we could try," Caleb said slowly.

"Ki and Fletache and I won't be far away," Jessie promised. "I'm not saying you'd need help or anything like that, but if you should, we'd be ready."

"Well—" Caleb frowned.

"Come on, Caleb!" Jeff urged. "We can bring it off, you and me! Let's help Miss Jessie all we can!"

"If we know what the tree thieves are planning to do, it will be much easier for us to stop them," Fletache said thoughtfully. "I would go myself, but as Jessie has said, it would mean much trouble if these people see me. They have no liking for me."

Caleb turned to Jessie and looked at her for a moment before saying, "All right, we'll do it. That is, if Jeff's sure he's able to go with me."

"Don't worry about me not being able," Jeff assured him. "This little scratch I got ain't such a much." He turned to Jessie and went on, "And don't you worry about me either, tomorrow night, Miss Jessie. I'll hold up my end all right."

"I'm sure you will." Jessie nodded. She turned to Ki and went on, "I don't see that we can make any sort of plan for the meeting, Ki."

"Neither do I," he admitted. "But at least we'll know more than we do now about what the timbermen are going to try."

"Oh, it won't be time wasted," Jessie agreed. "So now all we have to do is wait."

Chapter 11

"I don't suppose it's strange for me to feel a little bit funny, looking down on everything," Jessie told Ki. "But this isn't at all like looking downhill, or along the side of a butte, or into a valley. Why, I haven't climbed a tree since I was at Miss Booth's Academy!"

"And I doubt that you've ever climbed one like this before," Ki replied. "I've been up a few, when I was younger, but I never saw one to equal this one."

"And it's not at all the same as the view you get looking down from a tall building," Jessie went on. "Why, this is almost like the times I went up in Ted Sanders's balloon!"

Jessie and Ki were perched high. The giant holly tree they'd chosen for their observation post was well inside the clear-cut area where the timbermen had put up their headquarters building. It was obvious at a glance that the holly tree had escaped being cut because the diameter of its massive main bole was too big for even the longest two-man felling saw to span, and the close-grained wood had proved too tough for the heavy axes wielded by the lumberjacks.

Shallow gashes in the thin bark of the holly's main trunk

showed where the axemen had tried vainly to chop into its seven-foot diameter. Many more, equally shallow gashes in the lowest branches also testified mutely to the choppers' defeat. Three branches rather than the more usual two formed the crotch, which occurred only four or five feet above the ground.

Not only its size, but the ease with which the holly tree could be climbed and the profusion of its large, thickly leaved branches, had drawn Jessie and Ki to the holly as soon as they'd come within sight of it. Not only did its heavily leaved branches offer concealment, but the low crotch gave easy access to the huge upper branches, which were larger in diameter than the trunks of many trees. Smaller limbs grew close together on the branches and formed a dense screen which shielded Jessie and Ki from sight. The massive holly tree stood in lonely isolation amid a wide expanse of pine stumps.

Dusk had been close when Jessie and Ki had approached the big holly tree after circling through the dense undergrowth. Fletache had found a suitable hiding place for himself in the thick brush beyond the cut-over area. They'd chosen the holly as their observation point, seeing instantly that its low-spreading foliage provided such an effective shield, while its first crotch could be easily reached from the ground.

Now they had climbed out on one of the sturdy limbs just above the second crotch, which occurred only head-high above the first. They sat crouched down, not only to be less conspicuous, but to be able to peer at the cut-over area through the swaying tips of the smaller branches that shielded them. They were now watching the stump-dotted expanse where the crowd of Thicket dwellers had been growing steadily larger.

Jessie could see very few differences among the men

that made up the growing group. Most of them were bearded and all were roughly dressed. About half of them wore bib overalls; the others favored either coarsely woven canvas trousers or blue denim Levi's jeans, though here in the Thicket where horses were rare and most of the travel was by boat or on foot there were no high-heeled cowboy boots in evidence.

There were very few who did not carry a rifle, though most of them soon set their long-guns aside, leaning them against one of the tall stumps. Pistols were few, but here and there a holstered revolver dangled from a gun belt. Two or three of the men wore battered derby hats, but equally battered, wide-brimmed straw hats predominated.

"I haven't seen Caleb and Jeff yet," Jessie remarked while she and Ki watched the growing throng of men walking around in the clearing.

"Neither have I," Ki told her. "But that's not surprising, with us up here looking through the leaves."

"I'm sure they must be here by now, though," Jessie went on. "Or will be very soon."

"Yes. Caleb didn't strike me as being the kind of man who'd break his word, once he's given it."

"Jeff would've found a way to get word to us if anything had happened to make Caleb change his mind."

Jessie nodded. Her eyes were moving across the milling group below, studying one and then another.

"That crowd keeps growing," she said after a moment. "If somebody doesn't call this meeting to order, or whatever they do with a crowd like this, those men are going to be too drunk to understand anything when the timber pirates finally get around to telling them what's ahead," Jessie said.

"We both know that's the whole idea," Ki told her. "The timbermen will encourage the Thicket people to get so drunk they can't think straight. Then they'll try to talk them into joining some kind of scheme that suits their own aims. The Thicket men will feel they've got to keep whatever promises they've made, and— Well, you know what I'm getting at, Jessie."

"Of course. It's like a rigged auction sale, Ki. People get to bidding and raising their bids, and then whoever's been working with the auctioneer to raise the bids suddenly quits and the highest bidder's stuck."

"We're lucky that nobody's looked up here and seen us," Ki went on. "But I don't think we need to worry any longer; it'll be full dark in another ten or fifteen minutes. And they—" He broke off as a ripple of voices rose to fill the void of silence that had prevailed earlier.

He and Jessie gave their full attention to the ground below them now. A small parade of men carrying lanterns was coming from the big building that stood between the holly tree and the edge of the clearing. When the light-bearers placed the lanterns on the tables, the babbling voices, which had been thin and desultory before, rose in volume as the men from the Thicket moved to pack closely around the newcomers.

That the lumber thieves were planning to be in the Thicket for a long time was evident from the building they'd erected as their base of operations. The structure was a large one. Its raw pineboard walls rose fifty yards from the perimeter of the stump-dotted area, the stumps being all that remained of the giant loblolly pines that had been felled to provide the lumber used to build it. The headquarters building stood two stories high, and covered more ground than did the main building at the Circle Star. From the almost solid line of windows that girdled its upper floor, Jessie guessed that it must be used as a bunkhouse as well as an office.

Not only did the huge building look out of place in the Big Thicket because of its gleaming yellow newness, but the logged-over area also had an alien appearance. As Jessie and Ki had traveled into the Thicket's heart, they'd seen only three or four places such as this one, where clear-cut logging had left a wide area of flat-topped, knee-high stumps.

Most of the few dwellings that had been visible from the creeks or trails seemed to invite the privacy of a small cleared area hemmed in by trees and the thick, tangled brush. Almost without exception, the small patch of cleared land where a house stood had been created by felling only the two or three trees required to build the dwelling, and to clear enough space for a small garden.

Though Jessie and Ki had occupied their vantage point for an hour or less before the lanterns were brought out, the first of what was now a crowd numbering perhaps sixty or seventy had begun drifting in soon after their arrival. The men—Jessie and Ki had seen no women among them—had gathered in loose, gossipy clusters close to the tables that had been brought from the big building even before Jessie and Ki took up their watch. Now the tables were loaded with bottles and raffia-covered demijohns, and a three-gallon wooden keg stood on one of them.

Before the bottles and demijohns had been brought out and placed on the tables, the Thicket people had been inclined to clump into groups of three or four, but now the groups began breaking up as the men began a slow but general drift towards the tables.

For perhaps a half hour, until their first drinks had been gulped down and the liquor started showing its potency, the men crowding up to the tables had shared the bottles in orderly and friendly fashion. There had been bursts of laughter here and there, and occasionally old friends among the Thicket dwellers had greeted one another with boisterous shouts which soon became back-pounding, ribs-nudging conversation, and in some cases had come close to fisticuffs.

Now all the greetings had been exchanged and the men were devoting their attention to serious drinking. This also followed a pattern almost as stylized as a minuet. After tilting a bottle for a swallow or two, the drinker passed it on to his neighbor, who took a gulp and returned the bottle.

By now, however, the earlier amicable attitudes of the Thicket men were evaporating in proportion to the quantity of liquor an individual had consumed and the time required for the whiskey to take effect. Soon a man who'd been holding a bottle overlong found it grabbed without ceremony by a neighbor. The friendly companionship that had been evident at first was being replaced by snarls and an occasional scuffle.

"They're taking the bait," Jessie said. "My guess is that the men behind this won't show up for a while, though."

"My own guess is another half hour." Ki nodded. "They'll wait and let the Thicket men get drunk enough to listen without really understanding what the effects of their work will be, but before they've put away enough liquor to get mean."

"They're going to need a lot of workmen." Jessie frowned. "And I'm sure that's why the timber hogs are staging this."

"They'll need workmen and logging rights both," Ki said. "Though I don't suppose any of the people who live in the Thicket have a legal right to be occupying the land their houses are on. Still, the timber hogs are—"

Ki broke off short and gestured to Jessie. She'd been watching the scene below. Now she turned, her eyebrows raised in a silent question. Ki motioned toward three men who were making their way toward the holly tree. From the angle of their approach, Jessie guessed that they must have come from the headquarters building and circled wide through the cut-over area. Now they were heading in a straight line toward the holly tree.

"They can't have seen us, it's too dark up here where we are," Jessie said, dropping her voice almost to a whisper. "If they had, they'd be running instead of walking."

"No. I'm sure they haven't noticed us. And they won't unless we do something to attract their attention."

"We can stretch out along this branch," Jessie suggested. She moved slowly and cautiously to lie down on the broad limb, which was almost as wide as a railroad sleeping-car's berth. Ki swung himself into a similar position and the two lay motionless while the three men approaching came on until they'd reached the bole of the holly tree and stopped in the puddle of darkness beneath its spreading branches.

". . . glad you're satisfied, boss," one of them was saying. "But liquor's about the best magnet we've got to pull a bunch of these Thicket rats together when we want 'em."

"It's damn good whiskey," another of the trio observed. "A hell of a lot better than it needed to be."

Jessie frowned. The speaker was one whose voice she'd heard before, and very recently. Then the man's name popped into her mind. It was Flynn, the timber pirate who'd been at the cabin when Caleb and Snatcher brought her there. Before she could tell Ki that she'd identified one of the men below, the third of the trio spoke.

"Don't make the mistake of misjudging these Thicket rats, Flynn. Or you, either, Treat," he said. "Not all of them are deep-woods ignoramuses. Those who were born here, the second- and third-generation bunch, may be ignorant and without schooling. But if you knew the truth about some who came here to hide out from the law, or maybe to get away from a kind of life they didn't enjoy, I'm sure you'd be surprised."

"Maybe," Flynn replied. "But with all due respect to your judgment, Mr. Stone, you haven't had as much to do with these people as I have. Since I've been here, I've seen and talked to a lot of 'em, and there's not one who's impressed me yet."

"Don't forget, Flynn, that I've been spending my time for the last several days at the Land Office branch in Houston," Stone told him. "There are deeds and wills and other records there with names and remarks about the personal histories of some of the people who've become Thicket rats. And 'rats' is a hell of a loose word to use. It doesn't fit what the Land Office records show."

"Flynn and I have been wondering what you found out at the Land Office," Treat remarked. His voice showed clearly that he was miffed over Stone's failure to confide the results of his visit to Houston. "But we went ahead with the preparations for this—this gathering, just as you'd instructed us to."

"Be damned glad you did," Stone said. "Because some smart shyster lawyer's been stirring up a fuss. We've got to move fast if we're going to get the timber out of here."

"Who's the lawyer working for?" Treat asked. "I don't see any of these Thicket people hiring one."

"You haven't looked very closely, then," Stone told the man angrily. "It took me about half an hour to find out that it was the big Tonkawa and a woman, Jessica Starbuck, who hired the shyster. I've heard about her before. She's richer than hell. Alex Starbuck was her father, and she inherited everything he had. She can afford to mess around in deals that are none of her damn business."

"Wait a minute!" Treat said. "The other day when I was

going around getting the Thicket rats to come here tonight, I ran across a couple of them who'd grabbed a strange woman and were taking her to their cabin! Is there a chance she could've been this Starbuck dame?"

"It's not likely," Stone replied. "From what I gather, she spends her time on a big ranch called the Circle Star, way out in West Texas." He paused and went on, his voice thoughtful, "Still, she hired those shyster lawyers who're messing up our plans. You'd better do some more snooping, Treat. Find out. If it was the Starbuck woman, we can get rid of her mighty damned fast!"

In the concealment of the holly's shielding foliage, Ki nudged Jessie. When she bent her head close to him he whispered, "This man Stone has done his investigating well, Jessie. He is a dangerous opponent."

"No more dangerous than others we've had to deal with, Ki," she replied. "But we're going to have to move fast to keep ahead of him. We'll know just about how fast after we've heard what he has to say to these Thicket people."

They returned their attention to the men on the ground after their brief exchange, and were in time to hear Treat's next question to his employer.

"I guess the Tonkawa's pushing to hold on to the land he claims old Sam Houston gave him and his tribe?" Treat asked. "If you remember my reports, that's the story he came up with when our land agents tried to buy him out."

"This lawyer's using the same old yarn," Stone said. "But it was good enough to tie up the land transfers we need."

"I ain't one to say 'I told you so,' Mr. Stone," Flynn put in. "But you ought to've let my men get rid of the Tonkawa while we had the chance."

"Yes. You were right about that," Stone admitted. "But it still isn't too late. I want you to send a couple of your best men to wherever it is that redskin lives. Tell them to find the Tonkawa and not to come back until he's out of the way forever."

"I'll take care of it, Mr. Stone," Flynn promised. "And I'll find out about the woman, too. I'll get my boys out to look for both of 'em the first thing tomorrow."

"Tomorrow, hell!" Stone snapped. "Get them started as soon as we're finished here tonight!"

"Whatever you say, Mr. Stone," Flynn answered. "I'll see to it while you're talking to the Thicket rats."

"Good!" Stone replied. "By the time the Land Office gets around to doing anything, we'll have every tree in the Thicket cut and on the way east."

"What about grading?" Treat asked.

"We're not going to take time to send out timber cruisers to grade the trees. I want you to clear-cut, Treat. Raft the logs downriver to the Gulf right away. There'll be plenty of time to grade them when they get to my sawmills back east. Now, these Thicket rats ought to be drunk enough to agree to almost anything. Let's get out there and see if we can hire the hands we need to start cutting trees tomorrow."

As soon as Stone and his companions had gotten out of earshot, Jessie told Ki, "Well, we know exactly what we're up against now."

"I don't like the idea of your being a target, too, Jessie," Ki said soberly.

"It's not the first time," Jessie reminded him. "What I'm more concerned with right now is finding a way to stop that man Stone. There'll be a lot of people besides Fletache hurt if he's left alone to carry out his plans."

"Do you think the Thicket people will really hire out to him? Won't they see that if they help him by hiring on as loggers they'll just be destroying their own homes?"

"Some will, of course. But most of them are terribly poor, Ki. I'm sure there'll be a number of them who'll take Stone up on his offer. We'll have to stop them, of course." She frowned.

"How?"

"I don't know yet, Ki. Maybe Fletache can help. He ought to understand his neighbors well enough to give us some ideas."

"Then while Stone or Flynn or Treat start talking to the men who're here, we'd better climb down and go back to the cave. Fletache's probably there waiting for us by now."

"We don't have to leave yet," Jessie said. "I want to hear what this man Stone is going to promise these Thicket people. His men have already started to get them down by that center table. We'll have plenty of time to get away later."

They turned their attention to the clearing again. The men from the Thicket were being urged by Stone's employees to move toward a table a short distance from the big building, where Stone and Flynn and Treat were waiting.

A carbide lantern had been lighted, and its brilliant rays spread a glow over the stumped area around the table. Its brightness and the sight of the three well-dressed strangers proved to be a magnet more powerful than the proddings of the timber pirates. When all the Thicket men except for a few stragglers were assembled, Stone climbed up on the table and spread his arms, gesturing them to silence.

"Now, I know some of you men have earned good money working for me before," he began, "and now I'm going to give you a chance to make a whole lot more. All of you know how to swing an axe and ride a felling saw. What I'm setting out to do is a job that you people haven't had the time or the gear to handle. I'm going to hire any of you who want jobs to cut down a lot more trees so you'll have enough open land to put in the kind of farms you need here. Farms where you can grow real crops that'll bring you more cash money than you've ever dreamed about! And I'm going to do a lot more! I'm going to pay you better wages than you ever expected! Now, how does that sound to you?"

For a moment there was no response to the timber pirate's question. Jessie said to Ki, "He makes it sound very good, Ki. But he's not telling them the whole story. The Thicket won't produce paying crops for three or four years. Most of those poor fellows will be starved out before they can earn enough from a new farm to keep them alive."

"And in the meantime, Stone and his gang will have all the money from the timber," Ki replied. "Money that's really theirs, because if they've been here any length of time they've got squatters' rights to the land and everything that grows on it, trees or crops or anything else."

Before Jessie could reply, one of the men in the crowd called out, "You sure put out a good bunch of gab, mister! The trouble is, you ain't telling the truth! Them trees you figure to take, they're ours! You say you figure to take 'em off of our land, but you ain't said a word about paying us for 'em! Now, let's hear what you got to say about that!"

Another voice rose from the group. "Go ahead and talk some more! There's some of us that'd like to farm, but if you think you're gonna hornswoggle us, you got another think coming! We ain't as dumb as it looks like you figure we are!"

"That's Caleb talking!" Jessie exclaimed. "And I'm sure that Jeff's with him!"

A murmur rose from the crowd around the table on which Stone was standing. Stone stood looking out over the men gathered in front of him, but he said nothing.

Jessie turned to Ki and said, "Stone's underestimated these men, Ki. And he's the arrogant kind who won't back up. Let's get out of this tree fast. Unless I'm wrong, there's going to be real trouble before too long, and Jeff and Caleb might need our help. We'd better be free to move when it starts!"

Chapter 12

Jessie and Ki began edging along the holly tree's thickly leaved branches. They moved as fast as they dared through the darkness, which in the black shadows of the big tree's foliage was almost impenetrable. Reaching the high crotch, Jessie levered herself down to the massive lower limb and started working her way toward the triple trunk crotch. Ki followed her closely. Though the murmurs from the crowd were growing louder, they still heard nothing from Stone after they'd reached the three huge limbs which joined to form the crotch at the top of the main tree trunk.

When she'd reached that point, Jessie stopped and Ki halted beside her. He asked, "Why're you stopping, Jessie? Are you waiting for something else to happen? Just a minute ago you wanted to leave."

"That was my first thought, Ki, when it looked like there might be some trouble. Stone must've had the same idea I did, because he certainly stopped talking in a hurry. But he hasn't moved, so I guess he's going to say something more."

Ki peered through the small gaps in the holly leaves and said, "Yes, that's what seems to be happening."

"Let's wait here a minute," Jessie suggested. "I'm still curious to see how many of those men are going to take the jobs he offered."

"Do you think Stone has any choice, Jessie?"

"No. He's going to have to pay the Thicket men pretty well if he wants them to cut trees for him. But they might turn down his money. That will depend on how successful Caleb is in getting the Thicket men to come over to his side."

Stone was still standing, looking at the noisy, milling group of Thicket dwellers. Unexpectedly, he drew a revolver from a cross-draw holster that had been concealed by his coat, and fired twice into the air. The gunshots quieted the Thicket men; they quit shouting and arguing among themselves and stared at Stone.

"When I start to say something, I expect to finish it!" the lumber magnate said. He did not shout, though his voice showed that he was angry. "Now, I've offered you men good jobs! I've been paying loggers eighty cents an hour until now, and brush clearers have been getting fifty cents. Anybody who wants to work on this new job and agrees to stick with it until it's finished will draw a dollar an hour for logging and eighty cents for brush clearing."

A low murmur swept through the crowd like a rippling summer breeze, but none of the Thicket men spoke out.

Stone went on, "That's all I've got to say. If you men don't want to work, there's plenty down in Beaumont and Houston who do. I can bring a hundred men in here before the week's out, and unless you want the jobs I'm offering you, that's just exactly what I'll do. Now, you men think about that for a while. After you've figured out how much cash money you can make working for me, any of you who want to sign up, go over to the office right away and get in line!"

Once again the chatter of excited voices rose from the Thicket men. Stone jumped off the table, and Flynn and Treat moved quickly to join him. A few minutes earlier, the crowd had been packed solidly in front of the long trestle table which Stone had used for his platform. Now the men began to break into small groups, and a babble of excited voices rose through the quiet air.

"What do you think they're going to do?" Ki asked Jessie.

"I'm sure some of them will take Stone's money," she said. The thoughtful frown that had formed on her face was hidden by the darkness, but was reflected in her voice. "I'm curious to find out how many will and how many won't."

"None of them seems to be in a hurry to go to the office and sign up," Ki remarked as he scanned the clearing.

"Caleb and Jeff might be partly responsible for that. They've got a big crowd around them."

"I hadn't noticed them before," Ki said. "But you're right."

"There seem to be more of the men standing around them than are going over to the table to sign up with Stone," Jessie commented.

"Most of them are in that crowd between Caleb and Jeff and the sign-up table, though," Ki replied. "I suppose they're the ones who can't make up their minds."

"You're probably—" Jessie broke off as the sound of feet thunking on the ground below reached their ears. She leaned forward to see who was approaching. Stone and Flynn were only a few paces away from the inky blackness below the holly tree's wide-spreading foliage.

"And they're not likely to notice us, as dark as it is

under that tree," Stone was saying when the pair came within earshot. "I'm curious to see how many of them are stupid enough to take the deal I laid out for them."

"I guess it is the best place to watch without them seeing us," Flynn agreed.

Jessie leaned back against one of the big branches that formed the tree's triple crotch. Aided as it was by the darkness, the massive fork was big enough around to hide her from the ground. She looked at the two other huge branches in turn, but Ki was not on either of them. Worry surged into her mind for a moment, then receded as she realized that Ki must have climbed up to the higher fork to make their presence less obvious in case either of the approaching men happened to look up. She settled down to listen.

"Who was the man that started all the commotion while I was trying to talk a minute ago?" Stone asked as he and Flynn came to a stop in the black shadow that blotted the ground under the holly tree.

"I didn't get a good look at the one that started the fuss in the beginning, and I couldn't hear him clear enough to recognize him by his voice," Flynn replied. "There were too many of them standing around him. The other one was a fellow called Caleb."

"Caleb what?"

"I don't know what his last name is, Mr. Stone," Flynn confessed. "Matter of fact, I don't recall ever hearing it. But that's how these Thicket rats are. Half of 'em don't want anybody to know their names because they're here hiding out from the law. The other half have been here so long that they think everybody knows what their name is."

"Well, I want you to find out," Stone said. Then he went on quickly, "Or maybe you don't have to worry about finding it, at that. You know where he lives, I guess?"

"Sure. I stopped by his shack yesterday to tell him and his bunkmate to be sure to come listen to what you had to say this evening. They'd picked up—" He stopped short.

"What's the matter?" Stone asked.

"I just thought about something," Flynn replied. "This fellow Caleb's got a bunkmate named Snatcher—at least, that's what everybody calls him. And I haven't seen Snatcher with him this evening."

"Caleb's the name of the man I asked you about," Stone persisted. "What's the rest of it?"

"Damned if I know," Flynn confessed. "I don't think I've ever heard anybody call him anything except Caleb. But yesterday, when I stopped—"

"Never mind the details!" Stone snapped. "I don't trust that son of a bitch! I noticed the way these Thicket men were responding to him when he broke into my talk a while ago."

"Oh, I guess he's pretty well regarded," Flynn said. "And I've got to give him credit. He's done a good job on the few things I've hired him and Snatcher to take care of."

"He's worked for you before, then?"

"He has, and so has his partner. They work pretty well together. I've hired them on as guides now and again, when I'm going someplace in the Thicket that I'm not too well acquainted with. It bothers me a little about Snatcher not being with him tonight, but maybe he didn't come along because he wanted to have the woman all to himself for a while."

"That woman you think is the Starbuck dame?" Stone demanded sarcastically.

"I don't know anything about her," Flynn confessed. "Just a woman they had tied up and gagged in their cabin when I stopped by to tell them about the meeting tonight."

"You don't know where she came from?"

Flynn shook his head. "I could tell she wasn't one of the Thicket women. They've got their own look. This one looked like she might've come from outside."

"Did it occur to you that this Caleb and Snatcher might've kidnapped her from one of those little towns around the edge of the Thicket? Doucette or Kountze or someplace like that?" Stone asked, sarcasm still tingeing his words.

"I don't know where else they got her, because like I told you a minute ago, Mr. Stone, she had the look of somebody from outside."

"And it didn't enter your mind that if they'd kidnapped her there might be a sheriff or perhaps even a Texas Ranger coming into the Thicket to look for her? Dammit, Flynn! An outside lawman is the last person I want to have poking around here, asking questions!"

"They'd just be after Caleb and Snatcher if they did come in!" Flynn protested.

"And if they find that I've got crews out cutting timber, they just might want to see if we've got a logging permit!" Stone exploded. "Which we haven't! And I don't want to have to get one, because if I do, there'll be a state inspector come nosing around here. I don't intend to pay any attention to the damned logging laws."

"Nobody else does. That ought not—"

Stone broke in. "Listen to me, Flynn. You'd better understand exactly what I intend to do. Maybe if you get a clear picture of my plans you'll be able to handle your job better."

"I guess I will, at that," Flynn agreed.

When Jessie heard Stone's intention to disclose what he hoped to do, she edged closer to the triple fork in order not to miss anything. The spot into which she moved did not accommodate her as comfortably. She found that in order to hold her place she was forced to hook her calf over one of the big branches of the fork and lean forward. She shifted her weight gently, moving slowly, until she found her balance. Then she could lean forward and hear more clearly.

"It's as simple as one-two-three," Stone was saying to Flynn. "I'm going to have two crews. They'll start cutting in the middle of the Thicket and clear-cut every damn tree that's growing, in both directions to the edge. I've got bull-teams on the way. They'll follow the cutters, and as fast as the clean-up men lop off the branches the bull-prodders will skid the tree trunks to the closest creek. I'll float the logs down the creeks to the Neches and lash them into rafts in Sabine Bay. Then I'll send the rafts through Sabine Pass and into the Gulf as fast as I can. Once they're in salt water, I don't have to worry. Until then, I'm gambling every inch of the way. Now do you understand?"

"Sure," Flynn replied. "But even if a state inspector should come noseying around the Thicket, a little payoff ought to keep him quiet."

"Not if the Land Office comes up with that deed from Sam Houston to the Tonkawas. The damned redskins are getting better treatment than anybody else in Texas right now."

"I'll go back to Caleb's shanty tomorrow morning, then," Flynn suggested. "Chances are he and Snatcher have still got the woman there, so it's likely I'll have to take care of the men, too."

"Don't get too free with that pistol of yours in front of witnesses, Flynn," Stone cautioned. "There's not any law here in the Thicket, but you don't have to go far outside before you run into it."

"I never have let you down before, Mr. Stone," Flynn said. "I sure don't aim to start now."

"It might not be a bad idea for you to stay close to that Caleb fellow for a while," Stone went on. "See that he doesn't start any real trouble."

"I'll do that," Flynn promised. He started away from the tree.

"Wait a minute!" Stone commanded.

Flynn stopped at the edge of the shadow cast by the holly's widespread foliage. Stone stepped up beside him.

"Where are you going now?" the lumber magnate asked. "We've got business in the office."

"If you can put it off for a minute, I'd like to get close enough to Caleb to see what he's saying to those Thicket rats. I want to find out about his partner and that woman, anyhow."

"A good idea," Stone agreed. "I'll stay and watch a few minutes longer. I want to see how many men we're getting out of this bunch. They're starting to thin out a little already, now that the liquor's gone."

Jessie could not see Flynn leave, but she heard his footsteps thunking on the ground and fading away. Then Ki's whisper reached her ears.

"I'm going to follow Flynn," Ki told her. "He's the kind who'd prod Caleb into an argument just to have an excuse for shooting him. But I'll need to borrow your hat."

"My hat? Why, Ki?"

"There are still too many lanterns burning out there. I can only use *ninjitsu* where the stumps are thick, and if I need to get close to Flynn in a clear space I'll have to shade my face, or he'll notice my oriental features."

Jessie had removed her hat while Ki was speaking. She handed it to him and said, "I'll wait here. Don't waste any more time. I'd hate for anything to happen to Caleb, and that man Flynn is an unpredictable killer!"

Ki dropped to the ground. His sandal-shod feet made

only a whisper when he landed, and in a few seconds the darkness had swallowed him. Jessie looked at Stone. He was standing with his back to the holly's low trunk, looking out over the clear-cut area, silhouetted against the light of the lanterns.

Beyond him, several groups of the Thicket men were scattered around the clearing. Now and then one or two would leave the group they'd been with and move to another. Jessie could hear the murmur of their voices as an undertone, and she caught an occasional word or phrase when one of them spoke more loudly than usual in the heat of a discussion, but she could get no clear idea of how their arguments were going.

Glancing at Stone's outlined figure she suddenly realized how little distance separated them. She rose to a crouch on the broad triple crotch and then stood up carefully to keep her boot soles from slipping on the smooth bark of the holly tree. She was reaching for the higher crotch to pull herself up to the concealment of its deeper darkness when, despite her careful movements, one of her boots slid off the huge branch.

Jessie's efforts to hold on to the precarious grip she had on the upper branch were useless. She toppled to one side. Her hands were clawing at the upper fork, but they found nothing she could cling to. Her attempts to grab the huge limb on which she'd been poised fared little better.

She managed to crook one knee around the massive branch and throw an arm around it a bit higher up, but now she was hanging over the ground. Though she used all the strength of the lithe muscles of her arm and leg, she was still dangling helplessly when Stone turned and gazed up into the tree to find the source of the noises that had reached his ears.

"Who the hell are you?" he called. As he spoke, he was stepping closer to the huge bole of the holly tree.

Stone's move brought him within a half-dozen feet of Jessie. She looked down at his silhouetted figure and saw his right hand move to draw his gun from its shoulder holster.

In spite of being more than a little bit angry with her own miscalculations, Jessie's voice was level and self-possessed when she replied, "You won't need your gun. I'm losing my hold here and I've got to drop to the ground before I fall."

"A woman?" Stone exclaimed when he heard Jessie's voice. "What the hell—"

"I can't hold on any longer," Jessie broke in. Then she repeated, "I've got to drop!"

"All right, let go," Stone replied. He did not raise his voice, but it was as hard as his name. He made no move to put his pistol back in its holster, but kept it aimed at Jessie as he went on, "I'm a lot more interested in knowing who you are and what you're doing up in that tree than I am in shooting you. Not that I won't shoot if you try any funny tricks. Let go and come on down. I want to get a good, close look at you."

While Stone was still speaking, Jessie released her precarious hold. She dropped lightly to the ground in front of him. Landing on her feet, she straightened up and looked at him. He was staring at her, a puzzled frown on his face.

"You're certainly not a Thicket rat," he said. "Not by the way you talk or the way you look. But that's a very businesslike revolver I see in your holster. I suggest that you stand quite still and keep your hands motionless while I relieve you of any temptation to use it."

Jessie had no doubt that Stone would shoot if she disobeyed his instructions. She remained motionless while he reached over to lift her Colt from its holster and thrust it into his belt.

"Now," Stone went on, "let's take up where we left off. I want to know who you are, where you came from, and why you're here." He paused. Jessie was sure that he expected her to reply, but she knew too well that in her present precarious position the only edge she had—if, indeed, she had any edge at all—was to perplex Stone as much as possible and hope that Ki would return quickly. She said nothing, and kept her face immobile. It was a tactic she'd learned to use early in her struggles with the business problems that had been left to her to resolve after Alex Starbuck's death.

"I see," Stone said at last when Jessie remained silent. "You're forcing me to carry the load. Well, I'm used to doing that, and I have a feeling that you are, too. Am I correct in assuming that you're Jessica Starbuck?"

Jessie refused to fall into Stone's snare. There'd been many times in her dealings with business and legal opponents, as well as with adversaries far more dangerous, when she'd used the same bait he was trying now. She remained silent and kept her face expressionless, meeting Stone's eyes steadily in the dim light.

"Legally, silence implies consent," Stone went on when he saw that Jessie was not going to speak. "Not that I'm a stickler for legalities, Miss Starbuck. But I assume that since you've been perched in this tree, spying on me and listening to my plans, you've already discovered that."

Jessie continued to stay stubbornly silent, but her gaze at Stone was as firm and unremitting as his as he stared through the gloom at her.

He went on, "I don't enjoy using rough physical measures to force someone to tell me what I want to know, but I'm afraid that you leave me no choice. You will turn around and walk ahead of me to that building. There's a door in the center of it, you'll see it as we get closer. Now, turn around and move, Miss Starbuck."

Jessie turned around. Before she could take her first step she felt the hard muzzle of Stone's revolver prod her back. She started walking steadily toward the building.

Chapter 13

Ki stood at the edge of the little group of Thicket dwellers that had gathered around Caleb and Jeff Barkey. He'd moved up to the men very slowly, keeping the lights to his back to make him appear to them only as a dark silhouetted figure, and had approached with seeming aimlessness while making himself as inconspicuous as possible. One of the Thicket men was speaking as Ki came within earshot of the group, and while the others were listening to his harangue, Ki quietly and unobtrusively joined the dozen or so men.

". . . and anybody that's got enough sense to pound sand down a rabbit hole don't want the Thicket clear-cut," the man was saying vehemently. "The way it is now's the way it's always been. Outlanders lets us alone. That's why my pappy come here, and that's why I've stayed. Where in tunket would we go if we let that damn timber pirate scalp off our trees?"

"Tobiah's right," another of the group agreed. "And so is Caleb. We'd just be cutting off our nose to spite our face."

"I say we tell that fellow Stone to go chase hisself," another of the men broke in. "And take his tree scalpers along with him!"

"Now, hold up a minute!" Caleb broke in. "It looks to me like the best thing for us to do is just play it easy."

"Maybe you better come down to cases on that, Caleb," a man in the group broke in.

"Why, there ain't no call for us to go telling Stone that we won't work for him," Caleb said. "Let them that wants to take Stone's money go put their names down, or whatever he says for 'em to do. We'll just go our way and leave 'em be for now, but that don't mean we won't be stopping by to talk to 'em later on when they're sobered up, and Stone ain't around."

"Caleb's cut the shank meat clean to the bone," the man called Tobiah agreed. "Except he didn't go far enough. There's a whole passel of folks in the Thicket that needs the money Stone's holding out to us. What's to stop them from doing his dirty work for him?"

"That's right," another agreed. "Stone's got enough men to guard 'em while they're cutting our timber."

"We better figure out a way to stop Stone ourselves," one of them suggested. Ki recognized the speaker's voice —it was that of Jeff Barkey. "My grandpap fought with Sam Houston when his men whipped old Santa Ana, and there was a lot more soldiers in the Mexican army than there was in Sam's."

"All of us has got guns," another of the men said. "And there ain't a man jack of us that don't know how to use 'em."

Caleb spoke up again. "There's one sure thing about all this palaver we're making. It ain't going to amount to birdshit if we spend all our time blowing instead of doing something."

"Something like what?" one of the group asked.

"Like getting ourselves ready instead of lallygagging out here in the dark," Caleb replied. "Because if I know Stone, he won't waste no time."

Tobiah spoke up again. "I guess all of us knows that, even if it ain't real good to hear it said. We got to get ready, put somebody in charge and do what he tells us."

"Then I say we make Caleb the boss," one of the group said. "Anybody got a better notion?"

A general murmur of approval rippled through the group. Then one of the men spoke up above it: "Stone's men might not have us outgunned," he said. "But I bet that all of us put together ain't got as much powder and lead as his bunch has, and we damn sure ain't got enough cash money to buy enough if it comes down to a fight."

"That's gospel truth," another agreed. "And I don't see where we can look to get it, either."

Ki decided that it was time for him to speak up. "If some of you and your friends are short of ammunition, I'm sure Jessie Starbuck will see that you get all you need."

"Who?" one of the men asked.

At the same time another said, "Jessie Starbuck? Who's she?"

"I heered there was some woman with a funny name that come here with the big Tonkawa," still another volunteered. "But I can't see why she'd have any call to help us."

While the little group had been talking at one side of the clearing, Stone's men had gone to work on the tables, picking up the lanterns and extinguishing them one by one. The transition to almost total darkness had been so gradual that the Thicket people had not noticed it until they shifted their interest from Caleb to Ki. They began crowding up to him now, trying to get a clear look at his face under the wide brim of the hat he'd borrowed from Jessie. To show them he had nothing to hide, Ki took the hat off.

"Hell!" one of them snorted. "This fella don't even belong in the Thicket! He's some kinda damn Chinee!"

"That don't make no never-mind," Caleb broke in over the babble of talk that rose after Ki had removed the hat. "And I know who this man is. His name is Ki, and he works for Jessie Starbuck. Now, seeing as you just picked me to take this thing in hand, I guess I'd be the one to go talk to her."

A murmur of approval rose from the men gathered around Ki as they returned their attention to Caleb.

"I reckon you would, Caleb," one of them said. "We ain't got much time before we'll need some help. It looks like Stone's ready to git started right off, but we sure ain't."

"If your friends want Jessie's help, I'm sure they'll get it," Ki told Caleb. "But it's easy enough to find out right now. Jessie's been watching everything from that big holly tree on the other side of the clear-cut. She's still there, waiting for me. Why don't we go talk to her?"

"Lead the way," Caleb told him. "I'm right with you." He turned to the Thicket men and went on, "Any of you that wants to tag along with us is mighty welcome."

About half the men began pulling away from the group, murmuring excuses about having a long hike home. The half dozen who remained grabbed their rifles from the stumps where they'd been leaning and strung out in a scattered line between Ki and Caleb as they started toward the holly tree. The men who'd been clearing away the lanterns had finished their jobs now and had disappeared, and the groups that had stood here and there in the clear-cut had also joined the general exodus. Winding in and out among the waist-high stumps, the little procession reached the big holly in a few minutes.

"Jessie!" Ki called, standing beside the bole of the holly and trying to peer upward through its foliage. "These men live in the Thicket, and they're not going to fall in with Stone's plans! They're going to need some help, though. Come on down and listen to what they have to say!"

When a moment or two had passed without Jessie replying, Ki frowned and said to Caleb, "Either Jessie's gone somewhere, or she got tired and dropped off to sleep up there. I'm going up to take a look."

Without waiting for Caleb's reply, Ki leaped up into the triple crotch and started climbing higher. He reached the spot he and Jessie had occupied on the upper crotch and still did not see her. Ki's mind was working at high speed now. He started climbing down, and in the few moments that passed before he dropped the final five or six feet from the triple crotch to the ground, he'd reached a conclusion.

"Jessie wouldn't have left here by choice," he told Caleb as he dropped from the tree and landed springily on the ground. "And I'm sure she'd have come to get me if anything important had come up. There's only one answer left. Stone and his men must've spotted her and captured her."

"That makes good sense," Caleb agreed. "And it stands to reason that they got her over in their building yonder."

"Well, hell!" one of the Thicket men exclaimed. "It ain't but a step or two over there. Let's go git her!"

"Wait!" Ki said as the man who'd just spoken turned away and took a step toward the loggers' building. "It's not yet time to start fighting. We're not ready. Jessie will know that she won't be kept a prisoner long, and we need to plan before we begin to do anything."

"Looks to me like we got one," another of the Thicket

denizens said. "Them damn clear-cutters have got the lady that we're looking to for help. Seems to me like we oughta step over there and give 'em a chance to let her go peaceful, and if they don't, we start shooting."

"That's what they're very likely expecting you to do," Ki pointed out. "And they're quite likely ready. They'd be shooting from the building, with the walls protecting them. We'd be out here without any cover. We wouldn't last two minutes."

"I reckon you got something in mind?" another of the Thicket men asked.

"Yes," Ki answered quickly. "We must wait. When enough time has passed for them to feel safe, they'll get careless. Some of them will lay their guns aside and go to sleep. When they do that, they will blow out many of the lamps that are now burning. Then we can free Jessie without as much risk."

"Sounds sorta softheaded to me," snorted the man who'd suggested instant action.

"It don't to me," another spoke up. "I'd say the little fellow here's got it figured about right."

"You will do well to listen to him," came a man's voice from behind them. For a moment the men froze. Then almost as one they turned, raising their rifles as they moved. The voice had come from the darkness at the side of the giant holly, and when they saw that the speaker was Fletache, the men who'd started bringing up their weapons lowered them a bit sheepishly.

"I was wondering where you were, Fletache," Ki said as the giant Tonkawa stepped around the tree to join them. "But I didn't think you'd be far off."

"I wasn't, Ki. I knew that if I joined the others in the clearing, Stone would see me and there'd be trouble. I waited in the brush where I could see and hear. It didn't

151

occur to me that Stone would have a chance to take Jessie prisoner, or that he'd even consider doing such a thing, or I'd have found a place close to you."

"You saw Stone capture Jessie?" Ki asked.

"No, that I did not see, if it was what happened. But I saw her walking ahead of him to the building, and watched both of them go inside."

"I can't imagine her doing that willingly, after what we heard Stone and his men talking about before he got up and spoke to the men here," Ki said. "He must've been holding her at gunpoint if she went in there."

"It occurred to me that he might have been forcing her to go with him," Fletache agreed. "But I couldn't be sure. It would not have been possible for me to reach her in time, even if I had known."

Ki shook his head. "There's not even an outside chance that Jessie would've gone anywhere with Stone."

"And it looks like it's up to us to git her out," Caleb put in. "Even if it means we got to fight sorta one-sided."

"Perhaps we won't have to fight at all," Ki said. "At least in the way you mean, Caleb."

Caleb frowned. "I guess I don't follow you."

"There is a way of fighting that is taught in my homeland," Ki explained. "Those of us who know it have learned to move quietly, and use our hands to kill. We also have some silent weapons."

While he talked, Ki was slipping a *shuriken* from his vest pocket. He released it now, his target the bole of the giant holly. The throwing-blade whistled past Caleb's head and sliced into the tree. Caleb gazed at the polished blade in the dim light.

"That looked right purty," he told Ki. "But I don't guess it'd stop a man like a slug outta a gun."

"Take my blade from the tree," Ki suggested. "And feel how sharp its edges are."

Caleb stepped up to the holly and pulled at the embedded *shuriken*. When it did not come out of the wood as easily as he'd expected, he pulled harder. His thumb brushed the edge of the blade as his hand slipped free without budging it. He stuck the bleeding thumb in his mouth and held it for a moment, then took it out and rubbed it over his forefinger, wincing as the raw edges of the cut rasped against the hardened skin of his finger.

"Danged if I can yank that thing out," he said. "And I got to give it to you, Ki. It's sharp as any razor I ever nicked myself with and didn't know when I done it."

Ki stepped up to the tree trunk and, with the skill that came from long experience in handling his weapons, worked the embedded *shuriken* free. As he restored the blade to its case he turned back to Caleb.

"Getting Jessie away from Stone is my job," he said, addressing all the Thicket men through their leader. "Give me a half hour. If I do not return with her by then, you and your friends can attack the building if you still feel like it."

"All right," Caleb agreed. "I don't reckon you'd be wanting to face them men in there by yourself if you wasn't sure you knew what you're doing. Go ahead, give it a try."

Ki nodded and started toward the building. It looked more and more like a fortress as he drew closer to it. There were only a few lighted windows on the upper floor now, and only one on the ground floor. Ki headed toward it and circled around the edge of the pool of light that was shining from its unshaded pane. Pressing himself against the building wall, he peered inside.

Jessie was sitting in a chair across the room from the window. A rope circled her waist and rose in an X across her chest to a spiral around her throat. Another spiral had been looped tightly around her upper arms and brought down to lash her knees together, then tied off around her ankles. Ki recognized the binding at once, for it had originated in the Orient. Its loops were placed so that even the slightest move forward or sideways, or the tiniest motion of hands or feet, would tighten to choking force the loop that circled her neck.

Stone sat sprawled in an armchair a few feet away, and on one side of him Treat was perched in a straight chair. He spoke as Ki caught sight of him. His voice was low, muffled by the windowpane, but audible enough in the night's stillness.

"It doesn't look like she's going to say anything at all, Mr. Stone," he commented. "She's a real stubborn one."

"Oh, I've been too easy on her," Stone replied. He took a cigar from his coat pocket and flicked his thumbnail across the head of a match to light it. Through a cloud of smoke he went on, "She'll talk in a minute, as soon as I've got a bright coal on this cigar. I never saw a woman yet who could keep still when she felt the heat of a cigar coal coming close to her cheek."

"You'd really burn her face?" Treat asked.

"Damned right I would!" Stone snapped. "She wouldn't be the first one, either!"

Jessie had controlled her features when Stone first uttered his threat. Though she had no doubt that the lumberman was capable of carrying out the threat his words implied, she maintained her impassive expression.

Ki, watching and listening at the window, began planning the moves he would need to make when he dived through the glass to keep Stone from carrying out his threat.

Inside the room, Treat exclaimed, "But what can she tell

you that we don't already know? You said you got all the information there was about the Tonkawa's claim from the people at the Land Office branch in Houston!"

"It's been more than two weeks since I was there," Stone replied. "And she's only been here in the Thicket for a day or so, or I'd've heard about her from the men we pay to keep us up on what's happening. For all I know, she was at the Land Office after I was. Unless she got some good news there about the old land claim that damned Tonkawa swears old Sam Houston gave him, she sure as hell wouldn't've come here."

"I see what you're getting at." Treat nodded, hesitated for a moment, then went on, "You won't be needing me any longer tonight, then, will you?"

"What's the matter, Treat?" Stone asked mockingly. "Maybe you haven't got the stomach to stay in my outfit if a little thing like this upsets you."

"It—it isn't that," Treat replied. "I've still got to go tell the men what you want them to do tomorrow. If you expect them to bring in as much pitch-pine as you said we'll need, they'll have to get started earlier than usual."

"I suppose that's so," Stone agreed. "It's not all that easy to turn up good pitch-pine trees here in the Thicket, and I want them to have all they need to get the job done right. Run along, then. I'll take care of the Starbuck woman."

Treat wasted no time in obeying. He left the room without a backward glance. Stone had been holding his cigar clamped between his forefinger and thumb. He put it back between his lips and puffed, but the coal had died. Reaching into his coat pocket, he fumbled for a moment, then tried the pocket on the opposite side, but again brought out an empty hand.

"It seems you'll have a few more minutes to think

things over," he told Jessie. "For your sake, I hope you decide to be sensible and tell me what I want to know."

When Stone left the room, Ki wasted no time. His *bo* was in his hand before the lumberman closed the door, and with the skill of a master at *ninjitsu* he tapped the windowpane with a carefully controlled blow at its weakest point, dead center. With only a whisper of sound and without shattering, the glass cracked into jagged lines that ran to three of its four corners.

Pressing at the center of the crack, Ki managed to get his fingers into the gap created by his pressure. A sharp tug removed the triangle of glass and Ki let it slip to the ground outside the window. Reaching through the gap, he turned the latch and slid the windowpane up as high as it would go. Less than a minute after he'd first tapped the windowpane, he was in the room, slashing at Jessie's bonds with his razor-edged *tanto*.

"I'm going to need your help getting out the window, Ki," Jessie whispered as the ropes gave way to his quick cuts. "This rope's been so tight that I haven't any feeling in my legs and feet."

"Hold on to the windowsill when I lower you," Ki said when the last of the ropes fell away. "I'll follow you as fast as I can."

While he was lowering Jessie out the window, Ki heard Stone's footsteps thudding as the lumberman approached the door. He dived through the window, landed rolling, and hurried back to Jessie's side. She was clinging to the windowsill, trying to stamp her feet and restore feeling to them. Ki wasted no time with words. He picked Jessie up and started running just as Stone's angry and amazed shout sounded inside the room.

Before Stone could reach the window, Ki had carried Jessie beyond the edges of the glowing rectangle of light it cast on the ground outside. Stone's silhouette blotted out the light as Ki hurried on toward the waiting Thicket men.

"We haven't any time to waste," Jessie told them before any of them had a chance to speak. "But Stone's got a devilish new plan started, and we've got to make plans tonight to stop him."

"What sorta plans?" Caleb asked.

"There's no time now to explain," Jessie said. "I'll have to tell you later. Get all the Thicket men you can find and take them to your cabin. I'll tell all of you at the same time."

"My cabin would be closer," Fletache said quickly. "All the men know where it is." He turned to Caleb. "Bring them there, Caleb. I must stay with Jessie and Ki. They came here to help me, and I am responsible for their safety."

Louder noises were coming from the bunkhouse as Fletache spoke. Caleb and the few Thicket men who were still with him had caught the urgency in Jessie's voice and did not stop to argue. They began to move at once, the thunks of their footsteps loud when they first moved but quickly dying away in the darkness.

"You can let me down now, Ki," Jessie said. "I think I can walk again."

"Don't try." The speaker was Fletache. The big Tonkawa went on, "I'll carry you, Jessie."

Holding her in his arms as he would a baby, Fletache set off at a fast trot. Ki was at his heels. Behind them, the shouts of the loggers faded and died away as they fled through the protecting darkness.

★

Chapter 14

"We're far enough away from the loggers now," Jessie told Fletache after he'd carried her for a quarter of an hour. "And the feeling's come back to my legs. I can walk. You don't need to carry me any farther."

They were moving through a small clearing when Jessie spoke. Ki was leading the way, and he stopped when he heard Jessie's request. Fletache came to a halt as well, and let Jessie slide from his arms. Though the night was moonless, the stars were bright in a cloudless sky. Jessie took two or three experimental steps, stamping her booted feet on the soft ground to get all the feeling restored to her legs. Then she turned back to Ki and Fletache.

"You were a very good rescue team." She smiled. "I just hope that I won't need you again soon."

"We'll try to be on hand if you do," Ki replied. "But now we'd better be moving on before Stone's men catch up with us."

"I've had time to think since we've left the loggers' headquarters, Ki," Jessie said. "Stone's too smart to waste time and tire his men by sending them out to look for us in the dark. He'll be more interested in having them do the job he's putting them on tomorrow."

"What job is that, Jessie?" Fletache asked. "This is the second time you've mentioned Stone's plans, and I'm curious."

Instead of answering Fletache's question directly, Jessie asked, "How easy are pitch-pine trees to find in the Thicket?"

"That's an odd question to ask at such a time," the Tonkawa said, frowning. "Only a few are still left. Once they were very plentiful, but those of us who live here have cut too many of them. We strip their small branches to use for candles and we split their trunks for kindling wood. They start a fire very quickly."

"Yes, I know a little about them," Jessie said. "And I had an idea there might not be too many of them."

"We of the Thicket do not cut the pitch-pine trees now, Jessie," Fletache went on. "There are too few of them, so we take only the few branches we need. Then the trees will stay alive for us to harvest again. But why do you ask?"

"I didn't ask just to satisfy a sudden curiosity, Fletache. I heard Stone giving some orders to his main helper tonight while he had me tied up in his office. His crews will go out tomorrow looking for pitch-pine."

"To use for kindling!" Ki exclaimed. "That's all pitch-pine's good for! Jessie, Stone's planning to burn the houses the Thicket people live in!"

She nodded. "That's the idea I had, too, Ki. He's learned tonight that the people who live here aren't going to work for him if they have to clear-cut, so now he's planning to burn all the houses and force everyone out. Then he'll send his own crews out to scalp the Thicket bare."

"We'll have to stop him, then!" Fletache said angrily.

"That's my idea, too," Jessie said grimly. "We'll make our plans tonight and be ready to move tomorrow when his men go out to cut the pitch-pines. I'm sure you and your friends here will know where to find them faster than Stone's axemen."

"They will," Fletache agreed. "And Stone's men won't start out until late in the morning. We will get to the pines first; we Thicket people know just where they grow."

"I was sure you'd say something like that," she told the Tonkawa. Then she went on, "On the way to your house, do we go near the cave where you and Ki left me?"

"We can. Why?"

"Because I want my rifle and more ammunition for my Colt."

Fletache nodded. "Going by the cave will not delay us long. But I must warn you, there are no easy trails that we can take to save time, either to the cave or to my house."

"Can we get there before daylight?" Ki asked.

"If we move fast, we can."

"Let's get started, then," Jessie said. "We'll need our supplies, and if we're lucky no one will have bothered them. But the only way to learn that is to get there, so lead the way and we'll soon find out."

For the next half hour they followed Fletache, pushing as fast as they could through the darkness. It was not a silent journey. The Big Thicket's wild creatures were abroad in the darkness they favored. Several times they heard the distant yowling of coyotes. Now and then the brush rustled ahead of them as a deer or some other large animal made its way through the mazed undergrowth.

Once Fletache stopped short, and when Jessie peered past him she saw a vague doglike form slinking belly-down on the vestigial trail just ahead.

"Isn't that a wolf?" she asked the Tonkawa as the ghostly shape was lost in the darkness.

"Of course. There are still a few left in the Thicket, and some panthers as well."

"What else are we likely to run into?"

"Perhaps a bear, though there are not many of them left. The people in here hunt them even more than deer, because a family can live for a full winter on the meat of one bear."

"I'd as soon miss running into a bear if it's possible," Jessie said. "How far are we now from the cave?"

"We will be there very soon, and from the cave it is only another small way to my house. But first we must go to another place, where I leave my wives when I know I will be away for more than a day or two. They have been there since I started for your ranch looking for you, Jessie."

"But that's been several weeks." She frowned.

"Of course. There has not been time for me to go and take them to our home since we returned from the outside."

After a moment of hesitation, Jessie asked, "You did say 'wives' a minute ago, didn't you, Fletache?" When he nodded, she went on, "Do you mind telling me how many wives you have?"

"Three," he replied calmly. "One is old, much older than I am. I took her to be my third wife when her husband died. He was the last man of our tribe but me who had full Tonkawa blood."

"Then your other two wives are young?" Jessie asked.

Fletache nodded. "Yes. But neither has given me a boy-child. I need a son who will keep our tribe from vanishing when I die."

"But you're not an old man!" she protested.

"Young men die, too," he replied soberly. "Though such things are not pleasant to talk about."

"No," Jessie agreed. Then she asked, "How much farther is the cave, Fletache?"

"We are almost there. The big rock that covers it will be at the end of the rise we are now going up."

They trudged on in silence through the ghostly night, up the gently slanting ground. When the slope crested at a ridge and they stepped off its hump, their boot soles grated on solid rock. Fletache turned abruptly and for a hundred yards or so led them along the slope that bordered the rock. Then he made another abrupt turn, and now Jessie could see the curved line that marked the mouth of the cave from which she'd been kidnapped, an oval blot of darkness, denser than the night that surrounded them.

"We will go in the cave," Fletache told Jessie and Ki. "We do not have to worry about Stone's men yet, but we have no time to waste. Take time to pick out what you need from the bundles we carried here. We will still reach my house in time to make our plans."

They ducked into the cave's oval mouth. Once in its shelter Ki scraped his thumbnail across the head of the match he'd taken out while they were entering. He joined Jessie and Fletache in blinking for a moment while the pupils of their eyes adjusted to the sudden burst of light. Then he turned his attention at once to the little heap of canvas-wrapped bundles that were piled in the center of the cavern. Jessie's rifle rested at one side of the bundles.

"Nobody's been here since we unloaded the dugout," Ki said. "Everything's just as we left it."

"Then you can easily find what you wish to take," Fletache said. "Later, I will come back with my wives for what is left."

Although they broke down the big bundles as fast as they could, assembling packs of the items they would carry with them was time-consuming. They could sort through the big parcels only during the brief periods of light provided by the matches Ki struck at frequent intervals. By the time their job was finished and they emerged from the cave the sky in the east was gray with dawnlight. It brightened constantly as they moved on, following Fletache through the high, dense undergrowth that began at the edge of the little clearing.

As they moved through the brightening morning the character of the Thicket changed again. The dense underbrush that had surrounded the little clearing in front of the cave mouth gave way to a stand of towering blackjack oak. Long thick strands of gray-green Spanish moss draped the high branches of the trees, and between the trees head-high clumps of palmettos thrust up their wide fan-shaped leaves. The leaves grew as wide as a man's arms could spread, and hid the terrain ahead as effectively as though they'd been woven into a solid wall.

If Fletache was following a path as he led them on a winding course through the stand of palmettos, Jessie could not see it when she searched the grass-covered ground with her sharp eyes. The big Tonkawa did not hesitate, however. Though there was no visible trail for him to follow, he was obviously familiar with each turn and twist that had to be taken to reach their destination. He led them on their tortuous course for a half hour or more before he stopped. Jessie and Ki also halted, just in time to be surprised when Fletache threw back his head and let go a ululating cry that seemed to hang in the air minutes after he'd stopped sounding it.

A moment passed, then another, and just when Jessie had decided to ask Fletache what his call meant, a twin to his long-drawn cry sounded in reply.

"Good." Fletache nodded. "We can go ahead now. The

way is clear, and by the time we reach the traps, my wives will have made them harmless."

"Traps?" Ki asked.

"Man traps," Fletache replied. "Those who live in the Thicket would not harm my wives, but there are always outlaws hiding here. Sometimes they leave the Thicket to capture women from a farm or a little town, but too many times they take a woman from one of the houses in the Thicket. No woman is really safe from them here unless her man is close."

"That's why your wives hide when you're away, then?" Ki went on.

"Of course. Almost always the outlaws will kill a woman after they have used her."

"I think traps are a good precaution, Fletache," Jessie said. "We must be close now to the place where your wives are?"

"Very close. They will come to join us soon."

"We're not going to stay in the place where they were hiding?" Ki asked.

Fletache shook his head. "There would not be room. We will go to our home, where we will be comfortable, even if we only stay there a short time."

Fletache broke off when a rustling in the heavy brush reached their ears. Jessie and Ki swiveled around to look in the direction of the noises. A moment after they'd turned around the broad, head-high leaves of the palmettos swayed and parted, and a woman appeared. Two others followed her closely, and while the woman who'd emerged first was bowed by age and her face seamed with a network of deep wrinkles, the others both seemed ageless. They could have been anywhere from twenty to sixty.

All three wore ankle-length gingham dresses of the same style; the dresses varied only in the color and design of the fabric's printed pattern. They came up to where Fletache stood with Jessie and Ki and stopped, looking at the strangers.

"These are our friends," Fletache said to the women. "Ki and Miss Starbuck." Turning back to Jessie and Ki, he went on, "My wives' names are Mossa, Kahdle, and Potowe."

As Ki made a waist-bow, Jessie advanced to the three women, her hands outstretched. They hesitated for a moment, looking from one to the other, then each in turn grasped one of Jessie's hands and squeezed it gently. None of them spoke.

"We do not have guests often," Fletache explained. "They are a bit shy."

He said a few words in a language strange to both Jessie and Ki, though it had the gutturals and singsong cadence of many Indian languages. The women nodded and smiled, and then relieved Jessie and Ki of their loads. Then they turned and began walking at right angles to the direction from which Jessie, Ki, and Fletache had approached. Fletache gestured for Jessie and Ki to follow them.

Their walk was surprisingly short. They'd covered only a few hundred yards when Fletache's wives turned sharply and led them away from the trail they'd been following. They burst through the last thick line of palmettos, and suddenly they were at the edge of a small clearing, a hillock that rose like a low, gently rounded dome from the dense vegetation which encircled it.

On the top of the hillock there stood a large house with three small cabins dotted between it and a spacious barn. Coming on it so unexpectedly surprised both Jessie and Ki. They stopped to look before entering the clearing. Fletache and his wives stopped with them.

"My home," Fletache said. In spite of his efforts to

speak in a casual, offhand fashion, the pride he felt was evident.

Both Ki and Jessie understood the Tonkawa's pride. The house was tidily built, with stout split-log walls notched to fit closely together, the small cracks between them chinked with clay. The shakes that covered the roof had been split carefully and laid straight. The windows were framed four-square and had glass panes. Along one side of the house the roof had been extended to create a veranda. Equal care had been given to the construction of the three small cabins that stood in line beside it, though they were of board-and-battan construction and had neither verandas nor chimneys.

"It's a very fine house, Fletache," Ki said.

"Yes, I don't blame you for being proud of it," Jessie added. "But I don't see any of your friends waiting for us."

"They will be here," Fletache assured him. "They will not come out of their hiding places until they see us."

"There's one thing that puzzles me," Jessie went on. "What are the three small cabins for? Guests?"

Fletache shook his head. "No, Jessie. They are for my wives. In the old days we Tonkawas had only one wife and one big tipi. Then our women gave us more girl-babies than boys, and we took up a new way. A man having more than one wife made a tipi for each of them, and a wife came to her husband's tipi only when he invited her."

Jessie nodded. "Now I understand."

"My people's customs may die with me," Fletache said soberly. "But while I live I will honor them. Now, let us go up on the porch and rest and talk of more important things. Mossa and Kahdle and Potowe will cook our breakfast."

"Tell 'em to put a few more names in the pot, then," a man called from the brush behind them.

There was no mistaking whose voice called out. Jessie and Ki recognized Caleb's voice almost as soon as Fletache did. Then Caleb stepped out of the brush and started toward them. All around the clearing the underbrush quivered as the men from the Thicket left the places where they'd been concealed.

"Now that you finally got here, we got some idees about what we c'n do to git rid of that damn Stone and his scheme to cut the Thicket bald," Caleb told them. "That is, if you feel like listening."

"Of course we'll listen," Jessie assured him.

"We done a lot of confabulating while we was comin' here," Caleb went on. "There wasn't none of us felt like resting. We was too mad and worked up about that fellow Stone and them thugs he's hired."

"Then you have a plan?" Fletache broke in.

"Sure as shooting we have!" Caleb assured him. "And one that'll likely work."

"I will go and tell my women to make a breakfast big enough to feed all of us," Fletache went on. "And we will talk while we wait. Jessie has some ideas, too. Perhaps between us we can find the best answer."

As Fletache stepped to the door of his house, Jeff Barkey said, "There's got to be some way to cut that Stone off at his hip pockets. I growed up in the Thicket; so did my mammy and pappy before me. I aim to stay here long as I draw breath."

Jessie said quickly, "That's the way most of your friends feel, I'm sure, Jeff. And it's the way it should be."

"Well, let's hear your idees, Jessie," Caleb suggested. "Ladies first, like Mammy always told me. Besides, I already found out you're right smart. Besides, what I got to say can wait awhile."

"I suppose you know that Stone's given up his first idea, of hiring you men from the Thicket to do the logging?" Jessie began.

"Now where'd you hear that?" one of the men from Caleb's group asked. "That's why he thrown that shindy last night, to hire on hands to do his dirty work."

"He changed his mind fast when only a half dozen of you came up after the meeting to sign on for his jobs," Jessie said. "In fact, he got so mad he's worked up a scheme right now to burn all of you out."

Jessie was not prepared for the reaction she got from the Thicket men. The meeting erupted into a hubbub of voices as some turned to their neighbors and began talking while others exploded into angry shouts, addressed to nobody in particular, but simply to vent their anger. She raised her voice to a shout.

"Please!" she called. "We don't have much time! Let's get on with what we've got to do!"

Fletache hurried from the house, drawn by the hubbub. He raised his voice to a shout that drowned the confusion of voices which filled the usually quiet air.

"Listen to Jessie!" he urged. "And listen to Caleb when he talks! We have no time to waste!"

When the group had grown quiet, Jessie began, "We know that Stone plans to send his men out to burn every house in the Thicket." A buzz of voices burst out, and she raised her voice to override them. "Please! Listen first, then we'll all talk one at a time!" The men quickly fell silent.

Jessie went on, "We know that we can't go up against Stone's men in a showdown fight. A lot of them are gun hands, hired killers. But he's sending them out by themselves today, and they'll be going in different directions, one man, maybe two, looking for pitch-pines."

"And all we got to do is follow 'em," Caleb broke in. "We go after 'em and hog-tie 'em, then we go back and tend to that damned Stone!"

"We won't have time to get back there before they leave, Caleb," Jessie broke in when he paused. "But there are enough of us to divide up and watch around the edge of that clearing."

When Jessie paused for breath, Caleb broke in, "Looks like me and Jessie's come up with the same idee, except I figured to dog after 'em. Her way's better, though."

"It doesn't matter whose idea it is," Jessie said quickly. "The main thing is to make it work. Most of those gunmen will be too loaded down to get to their guns fast, so we ought to be able to handle them." She looked around the faces of the Thicket men and asked, "Do you think we can do it?"

Some of the Thicket men merely nodded. Others shouted their approval. Then Jeff Barkey called loudly, "We can do it or bust our britches trying! I say we work it out while we eat and then get back there and give those fellows the best what-for we got!"

His words were followed by a roar of agreement. As it died down, Fletache said, "There is no hurry. Breakfast is ready. We will eat and rest, and then we will move. By this time tomorrow we will be rid of Stone, and the Thicket will be our peaceful home again!"

Chapter 15

Though the breakfast prepared by Fletache's wives consisted of grits and fried salt hogback, it was the same meal that most of the Thicket men would have had at their own tables. While they ate, Jessie's plan was discussed and refined. Before the meal was finished, the men had paired up and chosen stations around the edges of the big clearing where Stone's headquarters building stood.

"Now we can rest until it is time to start back to where we will wait for the timber pirates," Fletache said as yawns began to break into the after-breakfast chatter. "I don't have room for all of you in my house, but the porch is large and so is the barn. I have spread fresh hay there."

"We'll make do," Caleb said. "Us Thicket folks has got used to taking care of ourselves; you know that, Fletache."

"And so have Ki and I," Jessie told him quickly. "We're used to shifting for ourselves."

"No!" Fletache objected. He glanced at the Thicket men, who were already starting to move, some heading for the barn, others to the veranda. Then he turned back to Jessie and said, "You and Ki have come here and put your

170

own business aside to help us. You are the honored guests of all of us in the Big Thicket. You will take the bedroom in the house, Jessie." He indicated one of the cabins and went on, "Ki, I think you will be comfortable in Mossa's cabin. She will be staying here in the house in case Jessie should need her."

Fletache's tone showed that he considered his decision to be one which allowed no room for argument.

Jessie said, "If that's what you insist on, Fletache. Thank you."

"Mossa will take you into the house and help you get settled in your room," the Tonkawa went on. "I will go with Ki."

As Jessie and Mossa left, Fletache led Ki to the nearest of the three cabins. As he opened the door, he said, "It is not like the house on the Circle Star, but it will be comfortable. Sleep well. We have a busy night ahead of us."

Ki nodded. "Thanks, Fletache. I don't think I'll need anybody to sing me to sleep, but I'll be ready to go when the time comes."

After he'd closed the door, the little, windowless building was almost as dark as if night prevailed outside. Ki stood motionless for a few moments, waiting for his eyes to adjust to what seemed to be the blackness of midnight after the bright sunshine outdoors.

As Ki's eyes became accustomed to the darkness, he could see that the cabin was furnished with only the barest essentials: a double bed, a chair, and a small nightstand. Even before he could see clearly, he'd become aware the little cabin was too warm for comfort. He pulled the sash of his loose black jacket free and tossed it on the chair, stepped out of his trousers and dropped them on top of the jacket, then tugged at the end of his *cachette* and unwound it to free his groin. Stepping into the bed, he stretched out. Within two minutes he was sound asleep.

Though the pressure of the hand that closed over Ki's mouth was gently soft, he snapped awake. Before his eyes were fully opened he had grabbed the hand with a *hiratetsukami* grip that brought a whimper of pain from the darkness. Then a woman's voice pitched only a breath louder than a whisper broke the silence of the dark room.

"Please! Do not hurt me!" she said. "I mean you no harm!"

Ki recognized the voice. It was that of Kahdle, the elder of Fletache's two young wives. Ki's vision had adjusted to the dark now. He released his grip and sat up in the bed. Kahdle stood beside it, looking down at him.

"I did not intend to surprise you so greatly," she went on. "But neither did I wish to disturb anyone outside."

"I'm sorry if I hurt you," Ki told her. "But I wasn't expecting anyone to come in here. Did you come to tell me it's time to get up?"

"No. There is much time left, and everyone is still sleeping. But from my room next door I saw Fletache bring you here, and it started me to thinking."

"Thinking? About what?" Ki suddenly became aware of his nakedness. He groped for the bedclothes, but Kahdle leaned down and caught his wrist and held it.

"You do not need to cover yourself," she said. "I have seen men naked before."

"Suppose you tell me why you came here," Ki suggested. "Do you need help in doing something?"

"I need help, yes," Kahdle replied. "But—" She stopped short.

By this time Ki's eyes had adjusted to the room's darkness, and he could see that Kahdle was staring at him.

When she did not go on, he suggested, "Maybe you'd better explain."

"Have you talked with Fletache as men talk together?"

"We've talked. But I'm not sure I understand exactly what you're trying to tell me."

"Men talk to men as women talk to women, without hiding what they feel," she said. "Has Fletache told you of his wish for a son, so that the Tonkawas might once more become a tribe?"

"He's mentioned it."

"But has he told you how many times he has lain with me and with Potowe, and even a few times with Mossa? And yet none of us has given him a child. We wives have talked about it together many times."

"Fletache didn't go that far when we were talking," Ki said. "But he'd talk a lot more freely to you, of course."

"Yes. So that is why I have come to you, Ki," Kahdle told him. "It is not easy to ask you, but I must. Will you give me the child that Fletache wants so much?"

Ki opened his mouth to reply, but closed it quickly. After the questions Kahdle had begun asking a few moments earlier he'd begun to form an idea of what she had in mind. He still had not arrived at a reply, and even now was unsure what his reply should be.

After a long silence he said, "Fletache would know."

"Yes." Kahdle nodded. "But he would not say anything."

"How can you be sure?"

"Mossa knows." While she was speaking, Kahdle was shrugging her shoulders out of the bodice of her long dress. She went on, "Fletache talks more freely to her than to me or Potowe. Mossa has the full old Tonkawa blood. I have some, but I am only half Tonkawa. I think that would be enough, though."

She let the dress ripple down her sides. As she moved, Ki could see her vaguely even in the darkness. Kahdle appeared as a half-embodied form against the cabin wall, an outline of small brightness broken by the dark rosettes of her small firm breasts above the spread of her hips and the dark shadow between them.

When Ki did not reply, Kahdle sat on the bed and leaned forward. She began to stroke his chest, softly at first; then, as her hand moved lower, her caresses grew more vigorous, and Ki responded to them. Though he could have controlled his response, he did not.

When Kahdle's hand reached his groin and began an even more intimate caressing he was half-erect, and her hand soon brought him up fully. Then she stretched out beside him and threw her thigh across his, and Ki was ready. He let himself think only of Kahdle's warm body and responded fully.

Even after they'd peaked and lain in silent fulfillment for a few moments, Kahdle held Ki to her. She locked her thighs on his hips and, after lying quietly for a short while, began a soft writhing beneath him that brought back his vigor. After Ki had met her silent urging and they'd peaked and passed the heights once more, she lay lax beneath him for several moments before slipping away and pulling on her dress.

For a moment the room was flooded with light. Then it was dark again as Kahdle shut the door. Ki stretched out and closed his eyes. Soon he was asleep.

"I'm sure all the men are in place by now," Jessie said to Ki without taking her eyes away from the perimeter of the stump-dotted cut-over area which they'd reached a half hour earlier. "But Stone's crews might've come back before we got in place."

"It's not likely," Ki replied. "From what Fletache told us, most of the pitch-pines are a pretty good distance from here. And except for this stretch they've logged off, Stone's crews won't know too much about the Thicket."

"Well, so far we haven't heard any shots fired," Jessie went on. "And I'm sure that we could expect that most of them would go for their guns the minute they saw any of our bunch."

For the past half hour Jessie and Ki had been in the shelter of a small stand of loblolly pines. They'd taken cover behind the deadfall that had formed when the lower branches of the tall trees broke from the trunks to form a confused crisscross maze. Through the years vines and creepers had coiled up the trees' dead branches until they formed an almost impenetrable screen. It was an ideal spot, one from which Jessie and Ki could watch the cut-over area with no danger that they could be seen by someone crossing the wide, treeless space.

They'd been brought alert several times. Once a deer took a half dozen dainty steps into the cut-over area before bouncing back into the thick growth when it faced the cleared ground and saw no brushy undergrowth ahead to protect it. A pair of squirrels had cavorted among the tall stumps for a few minutes before their antics carried them out of sight, and once they saw the brush at the edge of the cleared ground shaking vigorously as a bear skirted through the edge of the thick growth, giving them an occasional glimpse of its shining black coat.

"It's beginning to get dark, now that the sun's dropped behind the treetops," Jessie broke a long silence to observe. "Do you think we should stay here any longer?"

"Perhaps not," Ki answered. "But I'd really like to know how the others have come out. If they're all in places as dead as this one, we won't have much to show for all our waiting."

"I suppose we'd better hold out until dark," Jessie said. "At least we'll know we haven't—" She stopped short and gestured toward the screening brush on the opposite side, then went on, "Maybe I'm wrong, but look at those bushes shaking."

Ki had turned his eyes to the area Jessie indicated. He said, "You're right, and we did the right thing by waiting."

"We'll wait a bit longer," Jessie said. "If that's not another deer or some other big animal—" She stopped when two of Stone's men pushed into the open. Both carried bundles of long pitch-pine branches astraddle their shoulders. Jessie and Ki watched in motionless silence until the men were past the center of the clearing and beginning to angle toward the loggers' building. Then Jessie spoke again.

"There's not any question about who they are and where they're going."

"No," Ki agreed. "And we can get close to them if we dodge from one of those stumps to the next one."

They broke cover, moving with silent care from stump to stump, until they were within twenty or thirty feet of the pair.

"Do you want me to go first, or shall we both move at once?" Ki asked.

"Both at once." Jessie kept her eyes on the two men. Her voice showed her preoccupation with their quarry.

She stepped from behind the tree. Ki followed her, and with quick but careful steps they closed the distance between themselves and the timbermen. Ki looked questioningly at Jessie and she nodded. They needed no words after the many times they'd faced similar situations.

Jessie angled to one side of the two men, Ki to the other

side. They stepped quickly from the shield of one stump to the next and were within three or four steps of the loggers when one of the men suddenly turned to squirt out a jet of brown chewing-tobacco juice. Jessie had just stepped from the cover of a stump, and the man saw her. He choked on his chaw, and the warning cry he'd attempted became a meaningless, bubbling garble of noise.

"Stop where you are and get your hands up!" Jessie called.

Holstered revolvers swung from the belts of both loggers, but when they moved to draw Jessie put a bullet into the ground between the feet of one of them, and Ki spun the *shuriken* he'd been carrying ready in his hand. The man who'd been Jessie's target let his revolver drop when the dirt raised by her bullet spurted over his boot toes.

Ki's mark was the second logger's upper arm, but the razor-sharp blade went an inch or so wide and sliced into the man's pectoral muscle. His gun hand fell, his revolver dropped to the ground, and while his yell of pain and anger broke the air he was already clawing at the blade, trying to yank it free.

After Jessie's first sharp command neither she nor Ki spoke. The logger hit by Ki's *shuriken* got the blade out at last. It was followed by a gush of blood, and he clamped the hand of his uninjured arm over the cut to staunch the flow.

"I got to have a doctor fast!" he called to Jessie and Ki. "Else I'll stand here and bleed to death!"

"Just keep your hand over that cut and you'll last awhile longer," Jessie told him. Her voice was flat and held no pity.

"Who in hell are you, and why'd you jump—" the other man began. Then his eyes widened and he went on,

"You're the dame the boss had tied up in his office last night, I bet!"

"That's right," she replied.

"What'd Mr. Stone ever do to you?" the logger asked.

"I'm sure that's of no interest to you," Jessie replied. "And save your breath, because I won't answer any questions. Now both of you turn around and march the way Ki leads you."

"Where you going to take us?" the wounded man asked.

Neither Jessie nor Ki replied, but Jessie raised the muzzle of her Winchester. Both men turned then, with Ki leading them. Keeping a safe distance from them in case Jessie was forced to shoot again, Ki marched them toward the margin of the forested land surrounding the cut area.

Ki glanced over his shoulder now and then for a quick glance at the rim of the sun above the trees. Its position was his directional guide. A quarter hour of brisk walking brought them to the edge of the logged expanse, and five minutes later they saw Caleb and the men from the Thicket. They were standing in a rough circle around a dozen men who sat on the ground with outstretched legs and arms bound securely behind them.

Jessie saw among them the familiar faces of Treat and Flynn; the rest were rough-looking strangers. There were more welcoming smiles from the familiar faces in the little group of Thicket dwellers who stood guard over the prisoners. Among them she recognized Fletache and his wives, Caleb, Jeff Barkey, Tobiah, and others.

Caleb came to meet Jessie and Ki. As he drew closer he said, "From what those fellows we've already caught tell me, you're bringing in the last of Stone's loggers. Not one of 'em got away from us, Jessie."

"What about Stone?" Jessie asked.

"Now that we've got his men, it sure oughta not be much of a job for us to grab him," Caleb replied.

"I don't imagine he'll give you any trouble," Ki said. "If you parade his men in front of that building he put up, he'll see that he'll have to give up his scheme."

"But supposin' he just goes outside of the Thicket and hires him a new bunch and comes back to try again?" Caleb frowned.

"I think we can kill two birds with one—" Jessie stopped short as an impish smile lighted up her features. Then she went on, "Perhaps I ought to say we'll show Stone how to do two jobs at one time."

Caleb frowned. "I guess I don't know enough about outsidetalk, Jessie. Maybe you better tell me what you're gittin' at."

"Instead of telling you, perhaps it'll be easier to show you," she told him. "Will you and your friends trust somebody from outside the Thicket to do that, Caleb?"

"Shucks, Jessie! You ain't no outsider now! I hear you got a pretty good ranch someplace out on the West Texas desert, but if anything was to ever go wrong, you'd sure be welcome to come settle in the Big Thicket and live with us!"

"Thank you, Caleb!" Jessie said. There was no mistaking the sincerity in her voice. "If you'll just get your friends to make the prisoners pick up those bundles of pitch-pine and keep an eye on them while everybody follows Ki and me, I think we'll find that we can handle Stone very easily."

Caleb had stared at Jessie for a moment with his brows drawn together in puzzlement. Now a smile grew on his face. He said, "I think I got a good notion about what you're figuring to do, Jessie. I'll git 'em started movin'.

You and Ki jist lead the way and we'll follow you wherever you take us."

Within a matter of minutes the little procession had formed up and was moving. By now the Thicket men had realized what Jessie intended to do, and as she and Ki walked at the head of the procession they heard their muffled whispering behind them. As they neared the blind corner closest to them, Ki turned his eyes away from the sprawling structure to ask, "Are you sure about this, Jessie? Isn't it too risky? Too dangerous?"

"I was sure you'd understand right away what I've got in mind," Jessie said. "But I'd say it's not risky or dangerous. We'd need a force of trained men to attack the building, Ki. Even if Stone is alone inside it, I'm sure he has enough guns and ammunition to hold off an army. Bullets won't go through those log walls, and he could dodge from one window to another, firing at us, using a half-dozen guns to save reloading."

"But suppose we set the Thicket afire?"

"All the area around it's cleared, thanks to Stone and his loggers. There's no danger of the fire spreading."

They reached the big rectangular log building a few moments later. Even before they'd gotten within a hundred yards of it, Stone began firing at the procession, but even such a hardened criminal as he hesitated to shoot his own men. His hurried, long-range shots were wild, though one or two kicked up dirt within a yard or less of Jessie and Ki

Jessie turned to the Thicket men and, without slowing her steady pace, she raised her voice and called, "Keep Stone's men between you and the building while you take them close enough to toss those bundles of pitch-pine against the walls. Don't waste time trying to light them that'll be done soon enough."

As though they'd been training to do the job, the

Thicket men obeyed Jessie's instructions. Within minutes the prisoners had been marched around the building and had tossed the pitch-pine bundles at its base. Jessie moved with the procession, putting a slug from her Colt through every window where she saw Stone's moving form. As soon as the last bundle of the resin-heavy pine branches was in place, she led the little parade away at a half run.

Ki gave them a fifty-yard start, then took out his packet of pull-fire phosphor matches and yanked one from its sheath of abrasive cardboard. The match flared into flame. He dropped it into the loose bundle of pitch-pine at his feet. The resin-heavy sticks lighted at once and spread rapidly to those on either side. The logs used in the building's construction had not yet cured fully, and the heat brought big drops of resin oozing from them.

Tongues of fire ran from the pitch-pine, up the walls of the building. Within a few moments the wall nearest Ki was a solid mass of shooting tongues of flame. That was all Ki needed to see. He began running, not bothering to use the slow movements that *ninjitsu* required to make him virtually invisible.

Just as he reached the edge of the circle of light, Stone's rifle barked from inside the burning building. Ki dived to earth and lay flat as he wriggled *ninja*-style through the last few feet of the rectangle of light cast by the flames. Then he leaped to his feet again and ran to join Jessie and the Thicket men, who'd stopped in the darkness beyond the zone of light.

A shout rippled through the cluster of Thicket men as a yell sounded behind Ki. He turned to look. Silhouetted against the flames he saw Stone running toward him, moving as fast as he could with his hands held high above his head. He waited until Stone reached him and clamped the lumber pirate's wrists in a *hirate-tsukami* grip from which there was no escape.

As Ki began marching Stone toward the group of Thicket men, Jessie and Fletache came to meet him. The big Tonkawa said, "I will take care of this one, Ki. Tomorrow we will load him and his men into boats and take them down the river to Beaumont. We will turn him over to the sheriff there."

"Will there be room in one of the boats for Ki and me?" Jessie asked. "We've been away from the Circle Star a long time, and I need to get back there."

"For you and Ki there will be a special boat," Fletache said. "And I will paddle it myself, just as I did when we came here. But now I must take this crook to join his friends. We will arrange our leaving later."

As Fletache dragged Stone away, Jessie turned to Ki. "We can go now without worrying," she said. "We've helped Fletache and his friends, and Greg Hendricks will see that they get some kind of valid title to their land. But—" She paused and looked around at the edge of the thick forest, lighted by the flames of the still burning building. "But you know, I think I'll enjoy looking out the window of my bedroom at the Circle Star for the next few months and not seeing a tree anywhere in sight."

Watch for

LONE STAR AND THE SUICIDE SPREAD

seventy-fifth novel in the exciting
LONE STAR
series from Jove

coming in November!

☆ From the Creators of LONGARM ☆

The Wild West will never be the same!

LONE ☆ STAR

LONE STAR features the extraordinary and beautiful Jessica Starbuck and her loyal half-American, half-Japanese martial arts sidekick, Ki.

__ LONE STAR ON THE TREACHERY TRAIL #1	0-515-08708-4/$2.50
__ LONE STAR AND THE LAND GRABBERS #6	0-515-08258-9/$2.50
__ LONE STAR IN THE TALL TIMBER #7	0-515-07542-6/$2.50
__ LONE STAR AND THE DENVER MADAM #13	0-515-08219-8/$2.50
__ LONE STAR AND THE MEXICAN STANDOFF #15	0-515-07887-5/$2.50
__ LONE STAR AND THE BADLANDS WAR #16	0-515-08199-X/$2.50
__ LONE STAR AND THE AMARILLO RIFLES #29	0-515-08082-9/$2.50
__ LONE STAR AND THE GOLDEN MESA #33	0-515-08191-4/$2.50
__ LONE STAR AND THE TIMBERLAND TERROR #43	0-515-08496-4/$2.50
__ LONE STAR AND THE OREGON RAIL SABOTAGE #45	0-515-08570-7/$2.50
__ LONE STAR AND THE MISSION WAR #46	0-515-08581-2/$2.50
__ LONE STAR AND THE GUNPOWDER CURE #47	0-515-08608-8/$2.50
__ LONE STAR AND THE LAND BARONS #48	0-515-08649-5/$2.50

Please send the titles I've checked above. Mail orders to:

BERKLEY PUBLISHING GROUP
390 Murray Hill Pkwy., Dept. B
East Rutherford, NJ 07073

NAME _____

ADDRESS _____

CITY _____

STATE _____ ZIP _____

Please allow 6 weeks for delivery.
Prices are subject to change without notice.

POSTAGE & HANDLING:
$1.00 for one book, $.25 for each additional. Do not exceed $3.50.

BOOK TOTAL $_____

SHIPPING & HANDLING $_____

APPLICABLE SALES TAX $_____
(CA, NJ, NY, PA)

TOTAL AMOUNT DUE $_____
PAYABLE IN US FUNDS.
(No cash orders accepted.)

☆ From the Creators of LONGARM ☆

The Wild West will never be the same!

LONE ★ STAR

LONE STAR features the extraordinary and beautiful Jessica Starbuck and her loyal half-American half-Japanese martial arts sidekick, Ki.

_LONE STAR AND THE GULF PIRATES #49	0-515-08676-2/$2.75
_LONE STAR AND THE INDIAN REBELLION #50	0-515-08716-5/$2.75
_LONE STAR AND THE NEVADA MUSTANGS #51	0-515-08755-6/$2.75
_LONE STAR AND THE CON MAN'S RANSOM #52	0-515-08797-1/$2.75
_LONE STAR AND THE STAGECOACH WAR #53	0-515-08839-0/$2.75
_LONE STAR AND THE TWO GUN KID #54	0-515-08884-6/$2.75
_LONE STAR AND THE SIERRA SWINDLERS #55	0-515-08908-7/$2.75
_LONE STAR IN THE BIG HORN MOUNTAINS #56	0-515-08935-4/$2.75
_LONE STAR AND THE DEATH TRAIN #57	0-515-08960-5/$2.75
_LONE STAR AND THE RUSTLER'S AMBUSH #58	0-515-09008-5/$2.75
_LONE STAR AND THE TONG'S REVENGE #59	0-515-09057-3/$2.75
_LONE STAR AND THE OUTLAW POSSE #60	0-515-09114-6/$2.75
_LONE STAR AND THE SKY WARRIORS #61	0-515-09170-7/$2.75
_LONE STAR IN A RANGE WAR #62	0-515-09216-9/$2.75
_LONE STAR AND THE PHANTOM GUNMEN #63	0-515-09257-6/$2.75
_LONE STAR AND THE MONTANA LAND GRAB #64	0-515-09328-9/$2.75
_LONE STAR AND THE JAMES GANG'S LOOT #65	0-515-09379-3/$2.75
_LONE STAR AND THE MASTER OF DEATH #66	0-515-09446-3/$2.75
_LONE STAR AND THE CHEYENNE TRACKDOWN #67	0-515-09492-7/$2.75
_LONE STAR AND THE LOST GOLD MINE #68	0-515-09522-2/$2.75
_LONE STAR AND THE COMANCHEROS #69	0-515-09549-4/$2.75
_LONE STAR AND HICKOK'S GHOST #70	0-515-09586-9/$2.95
_LONE STAR AND THE DEADLY STRANGER #71	0-515-09648-2/$2.95
_LONE STAR AND THE SILVER BANDITS #72	0-515-09683-0/$2.95
_LONE STAR AND THE NEVADA BLOODBATH #73	0-515-09708-X/$2.95

Please send the titles I've checked above. Mail orders to:

BERKLEY PUBLISHING GROUP
390 Murray Hill Pkwy., Dept. B
East Rutherford, NJ 07073

NAME_____

ADDRESS_____

CITY_____

STATE_____ ZIP_____

Please allow 6 weeks for delivery.
Prices are subject to change without notice.

POSTAGE & HANDLING:
$1.00 for one book, $.25 for each additional. Do not exceed $3.50.

BOOK TOTAL $_____

SHIPPING & HANDLING $_____

APPLICABLE SALES TAX $_____
(CA, NJ, NY, PA)

TOTAL AMOUNT DUE $_____
PAYABLE IN US FUNDS.
(No cash orders accepted.)

LONGARM

Explore the exciting Old West with one of the men who made it wild!

_ 0-515-08796-3	LONGARM AND THE BONE SKINNERS #96	$2.75
_ 0-515-08838-2	LONGARM AND THE MEXICAN LINE-UP #97	$2.75
_ 0-515-08883-8	LONGARM AND THE TRAIL DRIVE SHAM #98	$2.75
_ 0-515-08907-9	LONGARM AND THE DESERT SPIRITS #99	$2.75
_ 0-515-09007-7	LONGARM AND THE DESPERATE MANHUNT #102	$2.75
_ 0-515-09056-5	LONGARM AND THE ROCKY MOUNTAIN CHASE #103	$2.75
_ 0-515-09169-3	LONGARM AND THE BIG POSSE #105	$2.75
_ 0-515-09215-0	LONGARM ON THE DEADMAN'S TRAIL #106	$2.75
_ 0-515-09256-8	LONGARM IN THE BIGHORN BASIN #107	$2.75
_ 0-515-09325-4	LONGARM AND THE BLOOD HARVEST #108	$2.75
_ 0-515-09378-5	LONGARM AND THE BLOODY TRACKDOWN #109	$2.75
_ 0-515-09445-5	LONGARM AND THE HANGMAN'S VENGEANCE #110	$2.75
_ 0-515-09491-9	LONGARM ON THE THUNDERBIRD RUN #111	$2.75
_ 0-515-09520-6	LONGARM AND THE UTAH KILLERS #112	$2.75
_ 0-515-09548-6	LONGARM IN THE BIG BURNOUT #113	$2.75
_ 0-515-09585-0	LONGARM AND THE QUIET GUNS #114	$2.95
_ 0-515-09647-4	LONGARM IN THE VALLEY OF DEATH #115	$2.95
_ 0-515-09682-2	LONGARM AND THE BLOOD BOUNTY #116	$2.95
_ 0-515-09707-1	LONGARM AND THE TREACHEROUS TRIAL #117	$2.95
_ 0-515-09758-6	LONGARM AND THE NEW MEXICO SHOOT-OUT #118	$2.95
_ 0-515-09807-8	LONGARM AND THE RENEGADE SERGEANT #119 (On sale Nov. '88)	$2.95
_ 0-515-09847-7	LONGARM AND THE SIERRA MADRES #120 (On sale Dec. '88)	$2.95
_ 0-515-09875-2	LONGARM AND THE MEDICINE WOLF #121 (On sale Jan. '89)	$2.95

Please send the titles I've checked above. Mail orders to

BERKLEY PUBLISHING GROUP
390 Murray Hill Pkwy., Dept. B
East Rutherford, NJ 07073

NAME _____

ADDRESS _____

CITY _____

STATE _____ ZIP _____

Please allow 6 weeks for delivery.
Prices are subject to change without notice.

POSTAGE & HANDLING
$1.00 for one book, $.25 for each additional. Do not exceed $3.50.

BOOK TOTAL $_____
SHIPPING & HANDLING $_____
APPLICABLE SALES TAX $_____
(CA, NJ, NY, PA)
TOTAL AMOUNT DUE $_____
PAYABLE IN US FUNDS
(No cash orders accepted.)

MEET STRINGER MacKAIL
NEWSMAN, GUNMAN, LADIES' MAN.

LOU CAMERON'S
STRINGER

*"STRINGER's the hardest ridin',
hardest fightin' and hardest lovin' hombre
I've had the pleasure of encountering
in quite a while."*
—Tabor Evans, author of the LONGARM series

It's the dawn of the twentieth century
and the Old West is drawing to a close. But for
Stringer MacKail, the shooting's just begun.

__0-441-79064-X	STRINGER	$2.75
__0-441-79022-4	STRINGER ON DEAD MAN'S RANGE #2	$2.75
__0-441-79074-7	STRINGER ON THE ASSASSINS' TRAIL #3	$2.75
__0-441-79078-X	STRINGER AND THE HANGMAN'S RODEO #4	$2.75
__1-55773-010-5	STRINGER AND THE WILD BUNCH #5	$2.75
__1-55773-028-8	STRINGER AND THE HANGING JUDGE #6	$2.75
__1-55773-051-2	STRINGER IN TOMBSTONE #7	$2.75
__1-55773-070-9	STRINGER AND THE DEADLY FLOOD #8	$2.95

Please send the titles I've checked above. Mail orders to:

BERKLEY PUBLISHING GROUP
390 Murray Hill Pkwy., Dept. B
East Rutherford, NJ 07073

NAME_____
ADDRESS_____
CITY_____
STATE_____ZIP_____

Please allow 6 weeks for delivery.
Prices are subject to change without notice.

POSTAGE & HANDLING:
$1.00 for one book, $.25 for each
additional. Do not exceed $3.50.

BOOK TOTAL $_____
SHIPPING & HANDLING $_____
APPLICABLE SALES TAX $_____
(CA, NJ, NY, PA)
TOTAL AMOUNT DUE $_____
PAYABLE IN US FUNDS.
(No cash orders accepted.)